This book has received many accolades in the short span of three years. First time was when **'Daily News & Analysis'** a leading English Daily Newspaper featured this book in their **'Time for Books'** section within a month of the book's release. Soon, the book caught the attention of the legendary actor **Mr. Amitabh Bachchan** and he wrote an emotional letter wishing the book success. Things didn't end here. The next was a letter from the **Hon'ble Union Minister Smt. Maneka Ghandhi.**

During this, the readers had started talking about the book, and the leading-edge author was interviewed by Radio One. The interview was aired for five continuous days and many times on the radio station..

The most recent one is from the king of romantic songs, **Ankit Tiwari (Music Composer and Singer),** who sent a message to the author on Instagram and called him for a personal meeting.

"Thank you for so thoughtfully sending me a copy of... 'I am a Saint And I have Paws'. The only creatures who have evolved to convey pure love are dogs and infants. Dogs do not become our whole life, they make our lives whole. Once you've had a wonderful pet dog – your life is never the same... ...wish your publication and your future efforts every success."

– Amitabh Bachchan (Actor)

"It is a valuable addition to my library."

– Maneka Sanjay Gandhi (Union Cabinet Minister of Women and Child Development)

"Just completed reading your book I am a Saint and I have paws. I must say it is so fresh, gripping and absolutely unputdownable. Wish you success for your book. You are truly the W. Bruce Cameron of India. Meet me someday..."

– Ankit Tiwari (Music Composer and Singer)

Every Dog Deserves A Home

"Dogs do not become our whole life, they make our lives whole."
- Amitabh Bachchan

Darpan Goyal

Invincible Publishers

First Printing: 2015, Notion Press

Second Printing: 2019, Invincible Publishers

ISBN: 978-93-89600-22-3

Invincible Publishers

Registered Address: 201A, SAS Tower, Sector 38,
Gurgaon - 122003

I dedicate this book to the saints in my life, my dogs – Faith and Elixir. This book would not have been conceived if they had not been in my life. Love you both…

Table of Contents

Saint was Abandoned

It was the month of May, in the scorching heat of the afternoon at around 2:00 pm, a large SUV halted at the far end of the highway. It was a high-end version of Scorpio with all windowpanes tinted dark. The lady in the passenger seat asked once again to the man driving, "Are you sure you want to do this? We can still try some other option." She didn't seem to agree with what the man, her husband, had decided. The plump man rubbed the thick gold chain adorning his neck; rolled down the windowpane, and spat the tobacco he was chewing.

"Enough is enough." He retorted in frustration. "I can't handle it anymore. The biggest problem today I have in my life is this mountain in our backseat. I never knew that a status symbol would cost me bloody more than the money." He glanced over his shoulders at the backseat.

"But…" She was interrupted; he didn't let her voice her concern.

"I have always given you a free hand to spend any amount of money on anything you want. But don't expect anything more from me, especially just for a dog."

The man pushed himself back, stretching his arms further back, and with an extended hand, he undid the left door of the passenger seat. He threw a big toy-ball far off and yelled, "Go! Go fetch it, baby, Go!"

What exited from the car was an enormous dog with long dangling ears and bright eyes; he ran for the ball. The dog was limping slightly from his hind legs, but nevertheless, he was extremely swift. And why wouldn't he be? The dog was playing his favorite game of 'fetch-the-ball'. In no time the dog got hold of the bouncing ball with his mouth, and with equal vigor ran back to the car.

But the car was nowhere around. The dog gazed in all the directions, then barked for some time, and later started to whine. Nothing happened. His bright eyes turned gloomy, he was sad, little scared, and completely confused.

The poor dog couldn't understand what had happened, and where the car had disappeared? He was to play fetch-the-ball game, but where was the master to take the ball back to? Who would now throw it back again for him to fetch? Where were the hands to stroke his head in appreciation? Where was the voice which would shout in excitement? Where had everything and everyone gone? It wasn't just the car or the master but a lot that was missing; for the dog.

The dog's feet felt the heat of the burning road. The Sun was high, he looked down at his own shadow; saliva dripped from his large flabby mouth, on his own shadow. The furry tail which was always held high and swished with a great deal of strength and vigor, was now tucked between his hind legs; the creature was now a little more scared.

His paws were inflamed, he started moving away from the road and got his soring feet onto the ground, which was comparatively less searing than the cobblestoned road strewn with charcoal. Alas, even there the scarce grass with short blades on the hard soil was hot enough to trouble the sensitive padding of its feet. He limped further deep on the mud road, took place under a tree. His eyes were looking all around with a mix of amusement, fear and anxiety. He remained that way for a couple of hours.

It was late in the evening, and the road was still completely deserted. All of a sudden, a car appeared, and the dog jumped with excitement. The dog thought, probably it was just a prank played on him, or he was left behind by mistake. As soon as he spotted the black Scorpio, he took off with high speed; he could have easily given a serious challenge to any Olympic sprinter. But the car didn't stop, neither did it slow down, and by the time the dog could reach the end of the road, the car was gone. He stood forlorn again on the road, the dog kept looking at the car disappearing and diminishing in size by every second. The smaller the car appeared, the more bewildered he felt.

Along with the sun, the hope of the master coming back for him was also going down. Yet, at the same time, the desire of meeting his master was as big as his 100kg body. Alas, little did he know that the wait would be much larger than his hope.

His trust in his master was so deep that he felt guilty of going under the shades. He was sure, because of him being away from the road, his master would have missed spotting him, and by the time he had made himself visible, his master had already whizzed past. For him, his master was in search of his four-legged buddy, with whom he had spent five long years. Approximately half of this dog's life span.

While the sunset, to some extent, had softened the torture of the heat, but at the same time because of lapse of time, the dog was quite hungry. He had never been on the road for such a long time in the last five years, and had no idea about how to find food? Because he had a habit of being served by his master. After the sunset with little time left for the night to fall, there was some movement of people; majorly labourers, probably going home after the day's work.

"Papa, Papa, see… The lion." A kid shouted who was seated on the cycle with his father, they were going home passing by the same spot where the dog was.

Shocked, the father halted the cycle and turned his eyes in the direction his son was pointing towards, he observed closely and told his son, "No beta, it's not a lion. It's a dog. And by almighty's grace, it is so big that it looks like a lion. He is surely somebody's pet! His owner must be nearby and will definitiley come to get him. Let's go home now. It's late, and your mother must be waiting for us."

Night had fallen, it was around 10:00 pm, the dog was starving, and the road was busier with people out of their houses for some post-dinner walks. Because of his size and his distinct looks (he looked like a lion), the dog had attracted a lot of attention. A crowd of people had gathered around him, which made him nervous; the dog had never seen so many strange faces staring at him. He went near the electric pole, lifted left hind leg and peed. Among the crowd, few had some knowledge about dogs' breeds, and they thought they knew everything about dogs. Such people were discussing and presenting their views (expert opinions) about the dog.

"Look he is peeing with one leg up. The dog is a male."

"I know baba, he is a SAINT BERNARD; one of the most expensive breeds in the world."

"It's not found here in India, he must be imported."

"But he is looking so bad; And has mud and sand all over his body."

"Look there, the fur is horrible at some places."

"I hope he doesn't stay here for long. He is dangerous for the kids."

"Not only kids, but he is also dangerous for everyone. That's why the owners must have dumped him." {*Dogs don't actually have owners, they have masters. Dogs are not a thing to be owned, they are pets who obey their masters. Masters are those who take care of a dog's food, love and safety. The life of a dog without a master is constantly under threat. Stray dogs follow one alpha dog amongst them, and this strong dog is the leader of the pack. But, abandoned dogs do not have a master or a leader.*}

"*Na re*, what dangerous? Just see how I manage him. You be ready with the mobile camera to click my pics with him, I will post it on Facebook."

This man raised some hope, but hardly had he taken a couple of steps towards his target, Saint Bernard yawned and the view of his massive, full and open, mouth revealing the semi-crooked teeth bracketing the slim long red tongue, made the brave boy fall back in sheer fear. The dog couldn't take it anymore; he started barking at the crowd, and in a short time everybody ran away leaving him alone.

Now, once again, the road was deserted, and the darkness of night made it quite scary. Once it was sure, as per the daily routine, that the humans won't come out of their homes, the other dogs charged in and surrounded this abandoned dog; the place was the territory of these stray dogs. {*Dogs being territorial animals do not allow any other stranger dogs in their territory. They consider the stranger as an intruder, like a thief in our house or terrorists in our country – all illegal entrants.*}

All these dogs barked at him and expressed their anger by baring their teeth in full glory. No botheration, he was not scared of the pitiable stray, street dogs. He had faced many such stray dogs during his morning and evening walks with his master, and was fully aware of the impact his size had on them. Saint Bernard just stood erect, with little trouble while lifting his hips, and barked thrice in full throttle. That was enough for all these dogs to run with their tails between their legs, and surrender their territory to him.

There are things about dogs which humans don't know for the simple reason that they have not been around dogs. There are things about humans which dogs can't tell because dogs don't judge humans without knowing them. The known fact by now was that this was a five year old GIANT male Saint Bernard, and the Saint was abandoned by the master (not the owner).

The Saint was abandoned.

The Soul of the Saint

It was the second day of the abandoned dog to be at the same place. He had come back to the roadside from the interior, occasionally scratching his neck, and was scanning the road for the car, the master's car, his master's car. People were going for their work and were passing through the same spot. Those people, who had missed seeing the Saint last evening were amazed to see such a magnificent statue. But none could fathom his eyes, the hope and curiosity in his eyes, his hunger, his thirst, and his sadness. The man with his son, who had spotted him the previous evening, was passing by the same place with few other laborers.

He was the first one to stop, so did his peers. He shared that he had seen the dog last evening as well.

"No one has come for him; probably the dog has lost his way." He was also concerned.

"There is no trace of any food around him, he isn't fed since the last evening; he must be hungry." He immediately decided to feed the dog one roti from his own lunch box.

"What will one roti be of use for such a big dog?" one of his friends stated. With little discussion and no persuasion, everyone decided to spare one roti each from their lunch boxes. They all were collecting the Rotis when something very strange, and apparently dangerous, happened.

One year old son of the laborer had approached the dog and was barely a foot away from the giant.

"Pappuuuu…." One of them shouted. Hearing his son's name being called out in panic, the father turned towards his cycle and saw it vacant; his son was not there. He immediately turned around to find that his son was standing next to the dog.

The dog smelled Pappu like a dog smells his food before eating. The hands of the father started trembling. Physically, Pappu was smaller than the face of the animal. Panic smitten father screamed for his son. The dog also panicked, and barked back loudly, that scared Pappu. The little boy started crying. The father enraged with fear, tried to shoo away the dog in a loud voice; the dog responded by barking louder, and this turned Pappu's weeping louder.

What they saw next froze everyone in their tracks; the father fell on his knees with tears rolling down his face. The dog was licking Pappu's tiny little feet and rubbing his tummy with the huge cold nose. Within seconds, the scared and weeping Pappu was rolling on the ground laughing delightedly. Licking of feet was comforting and the touch of cold nose tickled. {*When dogs are in the mood to get pampered they offer their tummy to be rubbed. A tummy rub provides immense pleasure to the dogs, and the bond between the one giving a rub and the dog deepens. Even mother dogs rub and lick the tummy of their puppies to clean and to show love.*

Additionally, there are other scientific reasons for mummy dogs to do so.}

The relieved father himself started to cry like a baby, whereas his baby was laughing like never before. The baby had probably never been tickled with something as cold as a dog's nose. His father started towards the dog to give him food, and take his kid with smiles mixed with tears, and then came the next shock.

The dog started to growl at the child's father. Saint Bernard bared his teeth, and placed one of his forelegs on the kid's lap, and continued to lick the kid's face along with the cold nose tummy rub. The dog was enjoying the kid's company and was not ready to part with. Nothing could be done except to wait and watch; everybody did just that. They were relaxed as they knew there was no danger to the kid from the dog, but they just could not understand why the dog was not allowing the man, with Rotis, to come near him. This was against the nature of dogs; they had seen and fed many on the streets.

Indeed the dog's behaviour was strange; he had never been like this. He loved humans a lot, and that was evident in his playfulness with the small child. Bright chances he wasn't willing to part with the kid; he was safe and felt joy with the kid. Neither the dog wanted food, nor he allowed someone to take the child away. He was strong enough, and all prepared to protect his new friend.

But after some time, when the kid started moving towards the father, the dog didn't stop him. He just watched the kid crawl towards his father. A tear rolled down from the father's still eyes, and also from the dog's eyes; though the dog licked it immediately as the tear reached the side of his nose. The father made a quick sprint and picked-up his boy and showered him with kisses. He was still holding Rotis in his hands for the dog. He again bravely took steps towards the dog and this time the dog was calm. He placed Rotis before him, but the dog did not even touch it. The man tried to stroke his head, but the dog turned away his head, indicating a clear 'NO' to the tender act. Finally, the man and the labourers started back for their work. However, before leaving, they vowed that every day they would pool in for the dog's food and serve him, whether he eats or not.

It was now the fourth day for the dog's abandonment, but no one had come for him. The only difference from day one to day four was that now there was a pile of food, yet he had not partaken any. The area around his black nose had scratch marks and pink patches; indicating some sort of infection. He scratched himself always and his hair looked shabby. A large, patched up umbrella was placed beside him. The umbrella was large enough to protect him from the heat of the sun, but he refused to sit in its shade, as he feared that his master might miss spotting him again, while on the lookout for him.

It was 2:00 pm, and the heat was scorching when a herd of cows passed by. The cows were seen running behind a man on a motorcycle, who was making a peculiar whistling sound that made all his cows follow him. The Saint perked his head up with some expectation, but the head soon reverted back to the earlier position: placed between his stretched forelegs. His eyes were just above the forelegs so that he could observe everything, and at the same time covered his nose and mouth to protect from the heat of direct sun.

Some cows were running fast, some were running slow, and few were walking lazily. Among the slowest ones, there was a large, white and brown colored, cow wandering on the path. The dog looked at her silently, and then the cow caught the sight of the food lying near the dog. She swiftly started to move towards the food, but before she could reach the dog began to bark. And did not allow the cow to enter his circle of territorial safe zone, marked around by his urine.

The cow stopped for a moment, and then lowered her head, displaying her big and sharp horns. She began to move her head ferociously to scare the dog. But the dog had seen many of such cows during his morning and evening walks; he knew, for sure, that there was nothing to be scared of. He barked loud and incessantly which finally made the cow turn and move away, and continue her journey of following the motorcycle man.

It was just then when the cow was out of sight that a calf came in the sight of the dog. The calf was walking extremely slow, struggling with each step, and then suddenly it fell by the roadside. The dog immediately got up and ran towards the calf. The calf was lying unconscious, dog looked around, but not a soul could be seen. He barked and sprinted in all directions to get some help, but all in vain; as if looking for a rose in a barren desert. Seeing no hope, he went back to his place and brought a roti for the calf. He sniffed the unconscious calf for some time and then started licking the calf frantically with saliva drooling all over the calf.

While the dog was giving his own treatment to the calf, the motorcycle man came back running looking for his lost calf. The dog was too occupied to realize the presence of that man and continued with what he was doing. The motorcycle man was startled by the scene; he had never heard of or witnessed anything of that sort in his lifetime. Without missing a minute, he pulled out his smartphone and started recording the dog licking the fainted calf. The calf probably had had a heat stroke, and because of the saliva of the dog, and the constant licking it finally got some respite. The calf recovered from his unconscious state and quickly ate the piece of *roti*.

It helped a lot, and finally, the calf was back on his feet. The motorcycle man stopped the recording and made the same whistling sound that was familiar to the calf, and the calf ran towards him. The man walked back to his motorcycle, watching his own recorded video. While they were walking, the calf looked back twice at the dog and mowed. The dog too gazed back for some time, then hung his head low and walked back to his place at a crawling pace.

The motorcycle man had a recording of something which could only be tagged as impossible. He shared the video in his WhatsApp groups and Facebook. Someone posted it on YouTube as well, and the video became viral in a day. It was no wonder that this video got a mention in the next day's local newspaper as well. Anybody and everybody who could read; read about it. Millions saw the video and Lacs compared the compassion of this animal with the behaviour of human beings towards the weak and needy. Media had named him Saint for his act of kindness; it was obviously derived from the name of his breed. And whenever he was being discussed, he was addressed as Saint and not a dog.

He was merely an animal, but a pious and evolved soul. With every passing moment, more and more people were becoming aware of this soul; the soul of the dog, the soul of Saint Bernard, the soul of a true saint.

The Soul of the Saint.

The Soul for the Saint

The news got many NGOs on their toes to rescue Saint, but there was an unanticipated problem, a severe one. Saint would not allow anyone to enter his territory. From the time he was abandoned, he was only a kid who had entered that circle, and a calf for whom Saint had left the circle. Every activist of every NGO there tried, but none could succeed.

A huge crowd had gathered around, Saint was looking at each face in the crowd with an expectation of spotting his master. As much as NGOs and animal lovers were disappointed with the failed attempts to enter his Zone, he was equally disappointed by not seeing his master in the crowd. He didn't want to be rescued; he wanted to go back to his master, to his home.

The wait was still on for him; a long and a tough one. He had lived a happy life so far, and when he needed the love and care the most, he was left to live the second half of his life alone. For him, there was absolutely no reason for his master to abandon him, and that's why he never believed that he had been abandoned. He firmly believed that he was just lost, and his master was surely looking everywhere for him. His hopes were high that the day will come when he will unite with his master and the family, his family.

On the Other Side

Pratima, a modern girl in her early twenties, was feeding the homemade 'chapati-mixed-milk' recipe to the street dogs in her society when her smart-phone rang. She ignored the phone until all the dogs had finished their food and took turns to lick her hands and face. Pratima was a fanatic dog lover. Many times her marriage proposals had been turned down because of her extensive love towards the dogs, especially the strays.

Her day started and ended with feeding the dogs on the roadsides. The rest of the day was spent in either taking street dogs to the vet for their treatment, or visiting homes of people for #house-check who wanted to adopt a rescued dog, or spending time with the rescued dogs being #fostered by Shivani till they found a permanent home. Pratima's parents never approved of what she was doing, but being a young rebel, she did what she felt right. But sadly, even her rebellion nature could not succeed to keep a dog at home, as a pet.

A rescued dog is generally left at the place where the dog has grown, as per the Indian constitution a street dog belongs to the street where it had grown. And any effort to re-locate, injure or kill the dog is a criminal offense, with a punishment of penalty and being put behind bars as well.

But in some cases the dog is so weak or in a condition that it cannot survive in the place where it belongs to, then it is taken away for treatment. Generally, there are shelter homes for dogs run by NGOs where these dogs are kept till their treatment and later put-up for adoption once they have fully recovered. Sometimes, when there are no shelter homes or no good shelter homes, the activist/ animal lovers/ dog lovers take these dogs to their home and take care of them till these dogs are completely healthy. Fostering is a term used for this activity where the dog is taken home and cared for some time. House-check is done to ensure that the dog once adopted will be happy with the family, mainly to check the fact that all the members of the family whole-heartedly willing to adopt.

Pratima called back on the number she had missed while feeding the dogs. It was a stranger. A girl who had called to inform that there was a pet dog who was always tied in the balcony of her neighboring apartment. She also told that this particular pet dog continuously barked and whined, but owners remained un-moved and left it always tied even in the afternoon. While the girl was worried about the dog, she was helpless to do anything about it. It was her friends who had referred Pratima's number to her.

Pratima's cheer after feeding the dogs turned into anger after hearing the news of this pet dog. Pratima got into her Audi, took out her diary, and noted the complete address along with the landmarks. Though the caller gave every bit of detail, she did not have the house number. She knew on which floor the dog was and, could point out the flat from the road, that's it. Available details were enough for Pratima to trace the house. She thanked the caller and disconnected the phone. Next, she immediately called up Kabeer.

Kabeer was yet another dog lover and was always ready to go to any extent, he could, for dogs. He was driving his black I-20 when his phone rang, he was about to answer when he saw that near a tea stall some people were playing mischief with a dog. He disconnected the phone with an instant message of "will call back later" and parked the car close to the tea stall.

Kabeer had worked with an MNC at a senior position before he quit his job and became a freelance consultant, to be more available for dogs in trouble. Kabeer carried a rugged look with full-grown un-trimmed beard and overgrown hair.

Kabeer came out of the car, he was in a red and white check shirt with khaki trouser, Woodland all weather shoes, and Rayban aviators. He moved towards the man who was kicking a weak street dog and kicked that man so hard on his hips that the man fell flat on the ground. Kabeer settled on his knees and pulled out a chew-stick from his pocket for the street dog that was being troubled. The dog was a female dog and was trembling in fear. She would not go to him, but as soon as the man got up and ran angrily towards the dog, she quickly ran towards Kabeer and hid in his arms. Kabeer gave her the chew-stick which she held in her mouth and moved at a distant place as Kabeer stood-up. The nasty man would have surely tried to hit Kabeer, but Kabeer's built stopped the man from getting physical.

The man angrily shouted, "Bastard… Are you mad or what? How dare you hit me?"

In response, Kabeer removed his Rayban glares and stared back right into his eyes and answered in a firm, but soft voice, "You asshole, whatever you were doing to that small puppy, I did the same to you. What's so fucking wrong in that… huh…? On the contrary, if I wanted to, I could have captured a video recording and dragged you to the police station to get you locked up under IPC Section 11(a) of PCA Act 1960."

Kabeer wore his Rayban back, took a cigarette from the tea stall and lit it. With first drag, he came back to the man who was still raging with his flaring nostrils. Kabeer spoke his final words before leaving, "Let me be very clear with you, I am letting you go away this time; next time it happens, you will have to bear much more pain, and in a lot more body parts. Got it?"

There was no response. Kabeer raised his voice, "DID YOU FUCKING GET IT OR NOT?"

The man felt embarrassed, everyone present there was looking at him. He just nodded in affirmation and left.

Kabeer's father was a senior High Court lawyer, who always supported Kabeer with his dog rescues, but never approved his rough way of tackling issues. Fortunately or unfortunately, his rough manner in handling complex cases always proved to be a great help, especially when he had the agenda of 'teaching a lesson'. And it was the only way he could rescue pets and tackle those who abused animals.

As soon as Kabeer turned to move back towards his car, he called back Pratima. Though behind his back some people appreciated what he had done, some others were condemning him for not minding his own business. Luckily, Kabeer had not heard it else he would have gone back and explained to them what his business was, and how nicely he minded it. When he heard the condition of the tied-up pet dog, he immediately ignited the engine and raced towards the spot where Pratima was waiting for him. They both got into her Audi and rushed towards the address.

It was around 4:00pm, and it was still hot. After a lot of turns into the lanes and narrow by lanes, they finally reached the location. They looked up towards the flat, and yes, a dog's head was visible, it was not making any noise. Kabeer observed that the dog was a furry breed. He also observed that it was a posh residential area, and the flat in that apartment block would cost nothing less than a crore. He was feeling disgusted that even people with financial resources do not take care of their own dogs.

Pratima removed her sandal and placed her barefoot on the road, and with-in seconds she pulled it off, "Damn! It's hot as hell, and the poor fellow is bearing this for no fault of his. He is in a condition worse than the street dogs; they can at least wander and find a place under some vehicle or a tree."

Kabeer also frowned taking off his Rayban, "That's the pity Prats (nickname of Pratima), those who take a dog as a pet, they owe the responsibility of taking care of them. Those dogs who are not pets their responsibility is taken by Mother Nature. Anyway, how long are we going to waste time here? Let's go and finish it off."

Pratima held Kabeer by his arm and told him in a firm tone, "I will do the talking first and..."

Kabeer interrupted her in a slightly irritated tone while moving towards the building, "Oh yes, *mummyji*. I will not say or do anything. What do you think I am? A nut? It's just that I quickly realize the kind of language the other person understands. And I talk in the same language. Now be quick."

Kabeer had spent more than a decade in the sales department of the corporate finance company. He grew from entry-level to senior management. He knew completely where to be polite, where to be educative, and where to be threatening and if required, where to be physical.

Kabeer and Pratima rang the doorbell, beside the nameplate of Mr and Mrs Jadeja, few times. Then a lady, dressed in a nighty, came out along with a small kid wearing only shorts. She looked to be in her late thirties, and the kid around seven years old. She looked at them with a frown, "No *bhai,* I do not want to buy anything, and you people should understand that in such hot weather you shouldn't be bothering in the afternoon."

"We are not selling anything. It is regarding your pet dog, and we want to talk to you about it."

To which the lady's frown turned into anger, and she exclaimed, "Ek kutte ke liye mere bachche ki neend kharab kari tumne (you disturbed my sleeping kid for a dog)?"

Kabeer took out his father's visiting card from his pocket and handed over to her, "I am his son, and if you don't allow us to help you, then the police will come to help the '*kutta*'."

Kabeer laid emphasis on the word 'kutta', which had annoyed him. He continued, "We are Animal Rights Activists and the way you are treating your '*kutta*' you can be put in jail, even for years. Now tell me, what's your preference? You want to talk to us or to the police?"

At the mention of the police, the lady got worried. She excused herself from changing the dress and called her husband to come home, explaining the scene in short. She was scared when she came back with a gown over her nighty and intentionally kept the doors ajar for her safety while allowing both of them inside.

As soon as Kabeer and Pratima entered, they asked her to bring the dog inside immediately. She was lost in thoughts just for a moment, when Pratima quickly sprinted towards the balcony, opened the door and unleashed the dog inside. Meanwhile, Kabeer instructed the boy, "*Beta* bring the dog's bowl and a bottle of fresh water along with a bottle of cold water, quickly."

Kabeer's commanding tone made the kid follow his instructions immediately without waiting for his mum's consent. By the time the dog came in, his bowl was already filled with fresh water. The dog finished full one litre of water and lay down on the floor. It was a German shepherd. Kabeer lifted the hind leg of the dog and looked at Pratima, "It's a girl." He checked further for signs of torture. Fortunately, there wasn't any. Pratima asked the lady, "Mam, what's her name?"

Mrs Jadeja replied, "Sweety. And she is very sweet."

Kabeer added info about Sweety to Pratima, "She is less than a year old."

Pratima, "Why do you tie her outside in this hot summer?"

Mrs Jadeja, "She doesn't allow us to sleep; she keeps on barking and barking."

Before the conversation could go any further, the man of the house entered and started questioning them, "Yes mister, who are you? How dare you enter my home? And what is this threat of police and all?"

Pratima got-up from her seat, but Kabeer didn't. Kabeer spread his legs wide and placed his hands behind his head. Kabeer's arms swelled up in this posture and tightened the shirt around his biceps.

Kabeer replied, "We are animal rights activists and have come to take away Sweety. We have enough reasons to believe that you are not taking proper care of her." Pratima knew that they would eventually take the dog along with them. But she wanted to have a discussion before that, to make it go smooth. And to avoid a scenario that was created, she wanted Kabeer to remain silent.

Mr Jadeja, "Why will you take her? She is our property, we have bought her for Rs. 40,000/-. And we will do whatever we want to do with her. If you want to call the police, then call them."

There was a small problem in calling the police. Though without a doubt, Sweety would be rescued, but she would be handed over to a shelter home, where she would not get the required love and care. For adult dogs, the management of such government aided shelters are suitable, but not for puppies, because the love and affection required by a puppy is not available in such shelter homes. Puppies rescued should go into foster homes for a better nurturing environment.

Kabeer from the same position replied, “Sir, first of all, a pet is never a property. Pet is a living being with life and emotions. And if you cannot take care of her, why do you want to keep her? Your wife told us that Sweety is a nuisance and keeps barking. You should be happy that somebody has come to save you from this botheration.”

Mr Jadeja, “Look mister whoever you are…”

Kabeer interrupted, “I am Kabeer! Kabeer Kapoor.”

Mr Jadeja, “OK! OK! So, Mr Kabeer Kapoor, I am not falling for your trick of taking my 40,000 rupees’ dog just like that. And who says we are not taking care of her. We feed her twice a day, and my son plays with her twice every day. We bought her for him only, she is his toy. And nobody can even dare to think of taking away my son’s toy… DO YOU UNDERSTAND?’ Mr Jadeja was now getting louder, and his tone was intimidating. “Madam, I am telling you very politely. Both of you get out of my house right now. Else I will have to throw both of you out of here.”

Now Kabeer got up from the sofa, “Look, Brother. I am trying to be very polite and make you understand. Though from your face, it is obvious that you won’t understand with words, still I am giving it a last try.”

Looking at Kabeer from close quarter made Mr Jadeja weak in his knees, he was no match for Kabeer’s stature.

Kabeer continued, “A dog is neither a property nor a toy. Though I am glad that you feed her timely and your son plays with her, but unfortunately that’s not enough. You people are actually not bad, but there is a severe lack of knowledge, and what’s threatening is, the complete absence of the required emotions, for her. She is a small girl, and your attitude is alarmingly harmful to her physical, mental and emotional health. You cannot take care of her, and you want her to take care of your son's playing needs? Absurd.

As of now, she is too small and somehow managing it out of her love towards you all, but with age, her health will deteriorate, and one day she will die. Then you will buy another dog as a toy for him, probably of some other breed because you would think that German Shepherd is a weak breed and dies soon. Rs. 40,000/- for a toy to survive for 3-4 years is too costly because every day's cost of food is also to be considered. And the vicious circle of your killing the dogs will never end.

It's better that you let us take her, and whenever your son wants to play with a dog, take him to your friend's home who has a dog. I am sure you 'bought' a dog because you were mesmerized by the way your friend's dog plays with your kid or his kid. Right?

By the way, what's the age of your friend's dog? Which breed?"

Mr Jadeja was in complete shock because Kabeer had stated exactly what had prompted him to buy a pet dog. But Mr Jadeja didn't know that most of the households have the same story for getting a dog. In an angry hoarse voice, he replied, "He also has a German Shepherd, Ricky. I don't know the age. But his size is bigger than that of Sweety."

Kabeer shrugged his head in complete despair, "Now you understand what the problem is? You don't even know the age of that dog. And I am dead sure that you have neither solicited his guidance on how to maintain a pet. Sweety must be vaccinated, but you never visited the doctor with her, if you had done so the doctor would have guided you.

You feed him what the pet shop sells you, also the quantity. This you do irrespective of the fact that every dog has different dietary needs, especially while growing. But you actually have not bought a dog, you have bought a toy; a toy that breathes, and walks." Kabeer instructed the son to pour the cold water into Sweety's bowl, and that kid again followed the instruction without waiting for any consent from his parents. Kabeer made the man take a look at Sweety, while she thirstily drank the entire litre of water again.

Kabeer again stood in front of the man and said, "She has consumed 2 litres of water in half an hour, guess how thirsty she must be? And in your daily routine, you would have kept her out in the balcony for another two hours or so, without water. Do you know what happens when water level dips in the body? Has your son ever fallen on the playground while playing? I am sure you would have never kept him without water that long in the hot sun. Do you remember how tensed you used to get when your kid would not stop crying? Why? Because when the energy level drops down the infant may die. Ever thought of Sweety, she keeps on barking for hours, and you know she is not even a year old.

Jadejaji, Sweety is not supposed to be a toy for your son; she is the younger sister to your son. And the best part is she would have indeed been a sister protecting her brother in all unfavorable conditions. Getting a dog is not about financial planning, '40000, 40000, 40000'. Getting a dog is about family planning. A member is added to the family and not a toy brought into your home. And I am sure you don't want to expand your family at this stage."

Kabeer turned towards Pratima and said, "Let's go with Sweety." Pratima picked-up Sweety in her arms.

Mr Jadeja and his entire family had by now realized their mistake and were feeling guilty to the core of their being. Their view of Sweety had changed, and they felt more connected emotionally. The family did not want to part with Sweety now, but the ego of Mr Jadeja was also not parting from him. With all his ego, Mr Jadeja stretched his arms to block Kabeer's way, and asked a question in a low voice, "What, if I don't allow you to take her?"

Kabeer folded the sleeves of his shirt to reveal Lord Shiva's tattoo on his forearm. He replied softly, "I do have other ways also to take her, don't force me to use those. It would not look good if a man gets beaten-up in front of his wife and son. Anyway, my quota of hitting people, for the day, is over."

Mr Jadeja suddenly broke into tears and fell at his feet. He cried, "Please don't take her, I have realized my mistake, and I will mend my ways. We all love her, and it's because of the limited information we had, that all these unfortunate things happened. I promise we will take complete care of her." Mr Jadeja almost snatched Sweety from Pratima's arms and started kissing Sweety all over her. He continued, "She is not just Sweety now; she is Sweety Jigarsinh Jadeja from today. If you want I will give you the key to my house, you can come anytime and do surprise checks on us. Please allow us to do the penance for the sin we have done. I beg you, please."

All this while, Sweety was looking at each one present, and trying to understand as what was happening there. She didn't realize that the fight was about her. The kid was standing behind his mother, and sobbing inconsolably over the news of Sweety's departure.

Mrs Jadeja with controlled emotions, but with a heavy heart, and teary eyes said, "We are glad that you came for her. I request you both with folded hands to give us one more chance; if you feel we can and will take care of her. If you still feel that we are not the right people for her then take her away. I can't be selfish anymore. Let her not be troubled anymore. Please do whatever is right and good for her, but also consider our request while making your decision."

Kabeer wiped a tear which has just reached his cheek and hugged Mr Jadeja. Pratima embraced Mrs Jadeja, and this time Mrs Jadeja broke into loud sobs, and the son too started to sob loudly. Before anyone could decide anything for Sweety; Sweety made her decision and began licking the son's tears lovingly. Everybody got into a group hug, and everybody respectfully agreed to Sweety's decision.

Then Kabeer gave the kid a Rs. 500/- note and requested him to bring a brick of Vanilla flavored ice-cream. Mr Jadeja immediately stopped his son and told Kabeer that they have it in their home. Half of the brick was served to Sweety, and the rest was shared by all and eaten with joy.

Kabeer and Pratima explained every big and small aspect to be taken care of and handed over a sheet with some basic details about pet care. They also mandated Jadeja's to visit Sweety's doctor. They said that the doctor might have a lot to reveal. Numbers were exchanged, and the duo left Jadeja's residence satisfied.

As soon as they entered the lift, Kabeer immediately expressed, "Pratima, we need to get back to the stranger who had informed you about Sweety and request her to keep you updated on the day to day happenings. Also we must visit them in next three days. They need to be on a regular check."

Though Kabeer had a hunch that it won't be required, still, Sweety was at stake so no chances could be taken. Pratima agreed and quickly saved the caller's number.

On the Highway

Meanwhile, the sun had set for the day, and Saint was in the same spot; he hadn't eaten a thing. The NGO volunteers had left, after trying their best. However, they had left a lot of dog food for him. As they were not allowed to enter his zone, they had to literally throw it as close to him as they possibly could.

For others, it was a roller coaster ride of emotions. At that juncture of time, everyone was concerned for Saint, everyone wanted to save him, and many wanted to adopt him, except one person who mattered to him; his master. The dog was stubborn; he wanted only his master and no one else. The news of him had spread like a fire in the jungle and had reached his master also.

The master was feeling bad and guilty, but now his pretentious honor and respect was at stake. He knew that if he went back, Saint would jump and joyfully come back with him, but that would also reveal him as the one who had abandoned Saint. Earlier people thought that the Saint was probably lost, but vets and the NGO had confirmed that the dog was actually abandoned, and he would only allow his master or master's family to come close to him. People's empathy for the 'worried master' had changed to myriad emotions of hatred, anger and disgust towards the 'master', the man who had abandoned Saint was now a guilty person.

A dog suffers because of a man's ego, but God has his way of taking care of all his children He has put on the planet. It was just a matter of time when Kabeer learnt about Saint. God had chosen Kabeer for the Saint. Yes, Kabeer was the soul for the Saint...

The Soul for the Saint.

Saint's Rescue

Kabeer and Pratima were driving back to the place where Kabeer had parked his car. There was a contented silence for the first few minutes, until Pratima spoke, "Kabeer, this was altogether a different kind of rescue, no?"

"Absolutely, and I feel that such rescues are much better than the rescues we have done so far. Now this man, this family, will be different and much better."

"I had no clue that people like them can also change; change their thoughts; change their feelings. It's a paradigm shift."

"You picked the right phrase. It's a PARADIGM shift; a complete transformation."

"Something like you went through, say a year back?"

"Close to a year, but not exactly so. I loved my dog. My transformation was for the strays and in-fact all other dogs, including others' pets also. I was over-possessive about my Faith (Kabeer's mix-Labrador's name). From the moment I picked him up in my arms, I forgot that he was a dog. For me he was like my own human child. And all other dogs were dogs…"

"Hmmm… When will my parents have this 'T' (referring to the word 'transition' as T) thing happening? When will I have my baby in my own home?"

Kabeer diverted Pratima's attention, "Just think of the kid yaar. He is so young, and the kind of growth he will have from here on, emotionally too. I doubt if he will ever be unhappy again in his life. At least till Sweety is alive. He has a sister now. Wow, this is so awesome. I pray that I get to do more of such rescues from now on."

Pratima, "You will Kabeer. And all the credit goes to you." Saying this, she pinched his arm.

Kabeer then said, "Not all the credit, but yes, my efforts are worth appreciating since I didn't follow your advice of keeping mum and let you do the talking. I just held a mirror to him, and he actually saw his dirty face. All the credit goes to them–for not denying the dirt, but actually making a decision of clearing that dirt. These people are awesome, but after all said and done, we need to follow the plan of surprise checks on them. Nothing should be left to chance. And..." Kabeer fell into an abrupt silence for some time. He was practically shaken by Pratima to bring him mentally back to the moment.

Pratima queried, "What now? What's on your mind? Where were you lost?"

"Home. Faith will again be upset with me. He will be able to easily smell Sweety from my clothes and will make faces, soon all his tantrums will start. It's now almost a daily routine, but he is still not ready to share me with the other dogs."

Pratima then countered, "Maybe that is because he doesn't feel that he is a dog, and he doesn't like dogs." And both of them laughed at this.

Finally, the two reached the place where Kabeer's car was parked, and he got into his car and drove home listening to songs played on the radio. He entered his apartment block and was just about to park, when he saw this familiar lady walking her dog. Suddenly the dog started to sprint towards his car. The lady in smart office formals struggled to hold the leash tight and keep pace with the speeding dog. She had to leave the leash and let the dog run freely. The dog ran with lightning speed towards his car, Kabeer stretched a little back and opened the rear door of his car, and the dog jumped right onto the seat like a trained tiger jumps through the ring in a circus.

The dog was Faith, and the lady was Meera, Kabeer's wife. Soon, she also came up to him and took the front seat of the car. She turned around and asked Kabeer, "So, how was it? And with whom is the dog now? Shivani?"

Kabeer, "No, she is still with her master."

Meera was puzzled and asked, "Why? How could you not do it? Were they like influential sort? How are we then going to rescue her…?"

Kabeer replied, "She is rescued and adopted by the same master and family."

Meera frowned, "Stop beating around the bush and spill the beans now. I don't like suspense, especially in such cases."

And then Kabeer narrated the entire incident while taking the duo on a drive. Faith, was least bothered about anything else when he was on a drive. The only thing which diverted Faith's attention was dogs on the streets. He would get agitated if he missed any chance of intimidating them with his loud barks.

As for Meera, the rescue story was so unbelievable that she actually texted Pratima to confirm if it truly happened. It was more unbelievable with Kabeer, and his rough and tough talk. Though, Meera knew quite well that below the rough-looking, almost ugly creature called Kabeer, there was a heart as soft as a mother's. Just like any protective mother, Kabeer too would turn into a fearsome Kaali whenever he saw a dog being mistreated. Kabeer had once been put in jail because he had broken the window of a Mercedes when he saw a dog locked inside the car. And his Papa (father) had come to his rescue.

Once they reached their home, Kabeer was greeted by his mother with a warm hug. By the time Kabeer freshened-up, his dinner was laid. Meera being a diet conscious person, skipped regular dinner and opted for salads and some milk. His mom always ate well in time to avoid the feeling of a heavy stomach at nights. Kabeer's father was out of town for some work.

Kabeer started his dinner with Faith. He ate one morsel himself and offered the other one to Faith, that's how they had their meals together. Faith was served food in his bowl only once a day, that too only when he was fed eggs. Meera being a Brahmin, had banned eggs in the house, but only for Faith, everything was allowed.

After the routine talks, Meera brought up the subject of a Saint Bernard been abandoned and all rescue attempts being failed. Kabeer decided to go and check on it the next day. When Meera showed the newspaper (Kabeer was never in the habit of reading newspapers) and the article about the video on Facebook, Kabeer got quite uncomfortable. He wanted to leave immediately, but he knew that if he did that, then it will actually be a Herculean task to make peace with Faith later.

After the meal, all retired for the day, but Kabeer had difficulty in sleeping. His mind was filled with mixed emotions. He felt good about Sweety's rescue, and at the same time sad about Saint's failed rescue. He had never seen a Saint Bernard in real life; neither did he know much about the breed. His curiosity and anxiety was so high that he actually spent the night tossing and turning around. Finally, he caught some sleep at 5 am in the morning, and at 6:00am Faith was ready for his morning walk.

He woke up, Kabeer with his heart melting licks. Kabeer had no choice; he got up and freshened up. By the time Kabeer was out of the washroom, the super-efficient dog was standing by the door, holding his body harness and leash in his mouth. This was the scene which created electric sparks in Kabeer's body even after a good night's sleep or night with no sleep.

Kabeer walked the dog on the road for his pee and poop, and back to the apartment block's garden for the fetch-the-ball game. Kabeer and Faith both loved this game. Faith used to get some target-oriented running, and for Kabeer, he just had to sit and throw the ball every time it was fetched back to him. Kabeer dropped a message to Pratima about the abandoned Saint Bernard. Her reply came after a while, as she was busy with her morning chore of feeding street dogs in her colony. Coincidentally she had also learnt about the Saint last night itself. They both then decided to start the day early. Luckily Pratima knew quite a bit about this breed, but she too had never seen a Saint Bernard in her life.

Kabeer got ready in an attire of Khaki cargo, which he wore for field rescue. He wore it along with a white golf t-shirt and grabbed a quick break-fast of stuffed '*aalo-parothas*' and '*lassi*'. When he left home, he met his father in the lift. His father was in his typical lawyer dress of white and black. Kabeer greeted him by touching his feet respectfully followed by a bear hug. Kabeer informed him quickly about the rescue work he was headed to. His father had also read about this dog. That was no surprise, as his father was like a 'newsaholic'. He could survive without a morsel of food for an extended period, but could never do without his daily dose of news every waking hour.

Kabeer reached Pratima's place, and she took her Range Rover for rescuing the big dog. Pratima was also dressed in a khaki cargo pants with a black and white check shirt and a jacket. On the way, Kabeer had called up Faith's vet, who also happened to be a vet for all the dogs rescued by Kabeer – Dr Divya. She had her own clinic and always treated rescued dogs without any fee. She never charged even a single penny from anyone who came with an Indian breed dog, be it rescued, adopted or owned, whatever the case may be. Divya knew everything about this breed as she had a few Saint Bernards as her patients and she promised to be at the site after her morning clinic routine. Dr Divya was married to a veterinary surgeon. They both had a shared passion for dogs. Though the surgeon was more emotional and Dr Divya more practical.

Kabeer and Pratima reached the spot where a small crowd of people from the neighborhood had already gathered. They both pushed their way through the crowd and saw this majestic creation of God. A giant lion looking dog was sitting there like an innocent kid with his forelegs stretched in the front, and his face hidden in the little space between them. With his hind legs also stretched backwards, he was almost six feet long, and a torso of minimum two feet diameter. Though of a giant proportion, but in that pose, he looked too cute, not at all the ferocious creature they both had imagined.

Pratima had thought it would be a cakewalk to rescue the Saint by some sweet talk and some warm gestures. That had been her modus operandi in the past seven odd years. Unlike her, Kabeer knew it won't be easy at all. It has been hardly a year for him to be a rescuer, but he was more of an observation based learner.

Pratima had just taken her first step towards the Saint when Kabeer stopped her by holding her arm. He pointed out towards the surrounding crowd and the food that was strewn everywhere, but not eaten. There were flies, mosquitoes and ants all over the food; and for sure on Saint's body too. The fur had become sticky at some places on his body, and every patch of white fur was full of mud and dirt. When Pratima saw the pitiable condition, she felt immense pain for the giant. Though she had rescued dogs even from the slimy gutters and the crowded slums and dingy potholes, she had never before seen such a beautiful creature in so much filth and dirt. It made her feel like crying.

At the same time, her seven years of experience was making her believe that she would be able to get to Saint in her stride easily, her mind was completely defying the fact that a day ago professionals and trained rescuers from registered, and the vintage NGOs had failed.

Pratima started to walk towards the dog, and this time she jerked off Kabeer's hand when he tried to stop her. Kabeer followed her, and as they reached the edge of the dog's territorial circle, the dog raised his head-up and frowned. She took one more step towards him, and he barked so loudly, that Pratima suddenly fell on the ground and froze in shock when she witnessed the sudden change in the dog. From a cute Saint, he had transformed into an intimidating one.

Even Kabeer felt a shiver go down his spine. The crowd was already standing quite far off, but still moved a couple of steps backwards, and some small kids ran away in fear. Kabeer was now sure that it would not be an easy task, but he also knew that it would be eventually done, though he did not know exactly how? Pratima actually had to be dragged out of that place by Kabeer and brought back to senses.

Pratima thought to herself that an expert could help in such a situation, else he would have to be put to sleep as Dr Divya said, "If a dog is not able to live a happy life for some reasons out of our control, then dog should be put to sleep." *{Put to sleep means mercy killing.}* But she did not dare to share this with Kabeer; she knew how much it pained him.

Kabeer got into a crawling position by lying down completely on his stomach, and he started to crawl towards Saint. He moved very slowly and kept observing the dog's reaction as he inched forward. The dog made a light growling sound, which made Kabeer realize that he was nearing his territory.

{Dogs are territorial animals and do not like intruders in their territory, especially other dogs. Dogs urinate on places with the purpose of marking the boundary of their territory. You may have seen that when dogs chase cars, they chase it to some length, and then stop. The place where they stop is the end of their territory.}

Now Kabeer's next movement made the dog bark loudly, but as soon as Kabeer pulled his arm back, the dog relaxed a bit. Kabeer swiftly took out his Swiss knife and drew a line on the ground. Then he got up and made another big line by extending it. This was like a '*laxman rekha*' for all, the territory which was till now only in the mind of the Saint had been made visible to everyone, and a strict instruction not to cross it.

Kabeer sat just outside the line with his legs crossed and started to observe Saint, or at least tried to observe him, as the dog had once again gone back to burying his head between his forelegs. By now, the sun was blazing hot, and the crowd had dispersed gradually. After about half an hour the place was utterly deserted with only one Range Rover, two people and a dog. The dog looked up at them, stared for some time and then finally dropped his head down.

Pratima and Kabeer were now feeling the heat of the sun, and trying to find a way out to help, but everything seemed impossible. How do they rescue the dog without getting near him?

This was an infrequent situation when Kabeer was in Sun without his Rayban. Pratima felt thirsty, she drank some water and offered it to Kabeer, but he denied and continued looking at Saint, and at the things strewn near him. He was keenly observing everything to find a clue. He was sure that some solution would be there, he just needs to focus.

Just then suddenly the dog pulled his head up again, Pratima was lost in her talks about what had to be done and how, but Kabeer continued his observation. Until now Saint had pulled his head up only when someone had made some movement, but this time there was no such movement, and yet the dog raised his head up. Kabeer narrowed his gaze on him and realized that he was not looking at them, but at something else on the road, and there was just a slight movement; a wagging of his tail. This was a good sign; wagging of the tail by a dog is an undeniable sign of the dog's happiness. However, why only a faint wag, which was barely perceptible? He informed Pratima about it, and then she too saw the same and observed it. Soon a car appeared, and the dog kept its gaze on it.

It was a Scorpio. Kabeer was left with some hope that probably the dog liked the Scorpio vehicle, and he could get him to get into the Scorpio easily. He turned to see that it was Dr Divya's car. Kabeer was so happy; he turned towards the dog, and cautiously, but deliberately entered the marked out area. Saint did not react, instead did not even notice him. But as the car approached nearer, the wagging of the tail increased a little more. But the moment the door opened, and Dr Divya stepped out, the wagging stopped; he got up and moved around rather uneasily. He shook his entire body in an attempt to get rid of the flies, and then went to a corner, peed and came back. He now realized that Kabeer was inside his zone, and made a low growling sound and moved his head slightly to suggest an impending attack. Kabeer got the message, and he swiftly stepped out of the marked area. Meanwhile, the Saint once again dropped down his body and sunk his head beneath the front legs – actually his hands.

Dr Divya, a middle age dynamic lady, petite in stature, was amazed to see the dog.

"OMG, I have never seen such a huge Saint Bernard."

She started sharing the facts with Kabeer and Pratima, "Either he is imported, or not bred in India, or both his parents were imported. He is actually the size found in cold freezing places, which is his natural habitat. This breed cannot bear the heat and catches a lot of diseases like asthma and heat stroke. He is surely suffering. His rage is also very unlike his breed, it's all due to the condition he is in. They are one of the most polite breeds; they are basically rescue dogs, rescuing travellers in the snowfalls. They are gobblers and eat a lot, but the food around him suggests that he is intentionally starving himself. This is not good; he will die a painful death if he doesn't eat soon. He has surely by now become a home for all the stray ticks. Firstly it's the season of ticks, and secondly, ticks are found in grassy areas and near trees. Kabeer, I know you don't like it, but if he is not rescued by this evening he will have to be put down.... You know what I mean."

Kabeer retaliated with barely controlled anger, "I don't know what the problem with you doctors is. Don't you veterinary doctors have to take that oath of trying your best to save lives, howsoever bad the condition maybe?"

Dr Divya replied calmly, "What we have learnt and completely agree with is that no animal should ever suffer." Dr Divya then shifted her eyes from Kabeer to Saint and continued, "Dogs deserve a good life and not a painful one. A dog's pain should end if that means ending its life." She then turned her eyes back to Kabeer and warned him, "Either you find some way of rescuing this animal or I shall have to find some way of... Even that won't be easy if he doesn't allow anyone to go near him. Maybe a shot or...." She shrugged her head in dismay and started to walk away with her final words, "Kabeer and Pratima, you know that I am just a call away if you ever need me."

Now the time had ticked past 2:00pm. It was over six days that the dog was abandoned. Kabeer was deeply distressed. He smoked continuously. He did not have his Rayban and no cap on his head too…The sweat trickling down his back was completely ignored. Only one thing was in his mind – how to win the trust of Saint. Only trust could help bring the rescuer get close to him and save his life.

Kabeer fetched his rescue bag and handed over his I-pad to Pratima, "Search every possible detail about the dog; every article, every photo, every video. Just keep saving it on the desktop, I swear on Shiva if this dog is put down, I will drag his master even from hell and tie him at the same place for fucking seven full days."

He fished out an unusually shaped cigarette from his bag and twisted the extra paper on the tip of the cigarette to cover the opening. He lit the cigarette; it took more than the usual time to light it, and he inhaled deep drags of the smoke. Even the color of the smoke was different from his usual cigarette. Yes, it was marijuana. He sat down and then crossed one leg over the other. He continued to take deep drags and stared directly at the sun. Tears started rolling from his eyes because of the direct sunlight and also because of the heaviness in his heart.

Pratima noticed his distress but chose to ignore and kept silently working on the task assigned to her. Pratima knew that the talk of putting the animal down had disturbed Kabeer tremendously. She also realized at the same time that it was clear that they could not allow the animal to die a painful death.

Kabeer knew only one thing, he had to rescue the dog, but 'HOW' was still an unanswered question.

Kabeer was now feeling much better as his brain was relaxed. He remained still for almost an hour or so until Pratima came and informed him that she had gone through and saved every possible piece of information available.

Kabeer took the I-pad and started going through the saved information. The pictures were of no use, the videos of NGOs activist trying to rescue were almost similar and looked repetitive he was almost about to log out when he saw the thumbnail of a video where the Saint was standing with his head down on the other side of the road. Thought was bright, 'This means that Saint had crossed the road and had come out of territorial zone.'

Kabeer immediately ran the video with an interested glint in his eyes, it was the video recorded by the milkman while Saint was licking the calf. He called out to Pratima, how could they have missed such a vital video. This was the very first video capture of Saint that made the breaking news of all the channels. It was this video that got the activists to try and rescue him. Somehow the failed rescues and the news of dog not willing to leave the place for anyone except the master became so huge, that this kind act of Saint was totally over-shadowed.

Kabeer realized that Saint had a heart of gold. He decided to go through everything all over again, so as not to miss any critical information. This video was something he had accidentally noticed, and later went through it in great detail; he could get some more important information if he thoroughly examined all the videos available. This strategy helped immensely.

He went over the news about a local who recounted how a one-year-old kid went to the dog and the giant dog played with him without hurting him. Also, there was a mention that the poor labourers were the first ones to give food to the dog. Kabeer saw a silver lining in the dark clouds.

He had two strong rays of hope. First, that Saint allowed an entry in his zone to play with a kid and secondly, it stepped out to help a calf. If he could get them repeated with some sort of trickery, then the Saint's trust could be won, and rescue operation could be carried out. He was so excited that though being a keen observer, he missed a point which Pratima had noticed, both the times Saint had made an exception for the young ones.

"Kabeer, both the incidents occurred on the second day of his struggle for survival, but now after almost a week of frustration and anger it would not be advisable to plan a trick using a kid or calf," Pratima suggested.

Kabeer agreed, "Saving one life by risking another does not make any sense at all."

It was almost 5:00 pm, and the sun was being a little kind. Pratima drank some water and offered to Kabeer as he had not taken a single sip since morning. Kabeer looked at the dog and said that even he must be thirsty. Food could be thrown at him, but how could one serve him water. Maybe he is just not eating, but would dearly want to drink water.

Kabeer quenched his full day's thirst and began to recall all the points about Saint that Pratima had furnished him with. Now it was dusk, and people started passing by the road returning from their work. He had given a list of things he would need to be brought by Pratima, while he chose to stay back.

Kabeer started interacting with every passerby, just to get hold of the man whose kid had developed a friendship with Saint. It was not difficult, and Kabeer soon was with the man and his son. He took all the details from him and noted that there was nothing new to be garnered. After sunset, it didn't take much time for the place to get dark. Pratima was back with all the stuff that he had asked for: a big food bowl, big water can and a bag full of delicious dog food.

Pratima told him that there were calls from her home and that she would have to leave now. He agreed. He knew that she lacked the support of her family. She had also travelled a great distance from the city to lend her support to a mad dog lover and a difficult giant dog. As Pratima left, Kabeer got a call from Meera. Meera was home and enquired about how long he would take to return home.

Kabeer was clear, "I am not coming back until I get the dog out of danger." This was not much welcomed by Meera and his parents. They argued with him for some time but at last, surrendered to Kabeer's decision.

Kabeer looked-up to the sky seeking help from Lord Shiva. The sky was getting cloudy on a full moon night. A deserted place lit by the moon and dark clouds floating over the moon made the deserted place quite scary. But being an ardent believer of Lord Shiva, he feared nothing.

Kabeer was very lucky to have a family which supported him with all his ventures, irrespective of the societal logic: be it his inter-caste marriage; delay in planning the family; going over-board to save dogs; standing for their fundamental rights or getting into dangerous fights with louts to protect women. He had been a madcap of a person, whose solutions to tough situations were risky but quick.

Suddenly the speed of the wind increased to the extent of a storm. Saint got up and started to bark in the direction of the wind. There was lightning which scared the dog, and he continued to bark at the sky. Other stray dogs also closed in sensing that the giant was scared, and they could get rid of him by hunting him down. However, Kabeer's presence was felt when he shouted with a strong, affirmative and loud voice: "NO!!!" All the dogs and the Saint looked at Kabeer, startled.

He tried to get close to Saint but was not allowed to do so. This was judged well by the other dogs, and they started to close in again on the Saint. Kabeer immediately moved out of the Saint's circle and moved around the circle towards the dogs to stop them from going any further. But there were too many dogs and attempting to enter the circle from all around, barking in a daunting way. Kabeer had to do something to stop them from attacking the Saint, but what could he do, he could not be everywhere around the big circle.

If Saint had allowed Kabeer to come near him, then the area to be protected would have been small enough for him to manage. But this difficult situation required some good wit and quick action. Something struck his mind; he opened the bag of dog food that Pratima had brought, went close to one of the dogs and squatted on his knees. The stray dog came to him and started eating the dog food hungrily. There was another lightning, and the Saint barked furiously at the other dogs and also at the sky. By now the rest of the dogs had entered the circle and were about to attack him when they saw Kabeer offering some food. They left the Saint unharmed and ran towards Kabeer. Kabeer sprinted far away from the Saint and attracted all the stray dogs towards him. He quickly scattered three packets of food on the ground so that every dog could get something to eat.

Once each one had tasted the delicious food, Kabeer opened yet another packet and started to feed them with his own hand one-by-one. He also embraced each dog while they were eating, then he stood up. When the dogs stood too for some more food, he instructed them to stay put. Few followed his instructions, few didn't. Those who sat back were the ones who got a second serving of the food and others were denied. Kabeer had used this strategy many times while settling a dog fight on the streets. He continued to offer the food to those who sat, and within no time, every dog was sitting and mouthing the food. Kabeer had taken the position of the master, the leader of the pack. He had lot of food to satisfy their hunger, and this also gave him sufficient time to become a complete master who could order the pack to follow his instructions. During these fifteen to twenty minutes, he just made them learn one command 'NO'.

The long-overdue rain started to pour water in drizzles with heavier lightning. Saint was in a whole awkward situation, which he had never experienced earlier. Saint was in a state of panic and was running like a maniac in circles inside his territorial zone, every lightning increased his fear. To cover him from the rain he was trying to hide below his own body, he knew nothing about handling this situation, he always had had a cover and people to protect.

His barks had turned into continuous whining and scared howls. Kabeer was in deep pain to see Saint like that, his throat painfully choked and inflaming eyes welled. Kabeer recalled when Faith was a puppy and was immensely scared with thunder sound he had heard the first time. Faith had burrowed himself in Kabeer's lap. Kabeer had hugged him tightly, and to soothe him, he had to keep on assuring with the words, "I AM HERE".

Kabeer wanted to run to Saint and hug him tightly, but Saint was now so panicky that he could have hurt Kabeer out of sheer fear. Kabeer was still a stranger and probably taken as a threat by Saint. Kabeer went near the circle, and the stray dogs started following him barking at Saint. Kabeer turned around and uttered a firm 'NO'. All the dogs stopped. Kabeer kept on saying 'NO' and kept on moving towards the Saint, being cautious not to enter the marked circle. Kabeer's little experience with dogs and huge corporate experience of keeping mind calm in nasty situations of the sudden crisis was incredibly helping him that night.

The rain got heavier and started to pour cats and dogs. The Saint was not at complete ease and was looking around in discomfort. All the stray dogs had gone in search of some shelter to sleep after a stomach full of great food. Kabeer remained seated at the border of the circle, getting drenched in the rain.

He had a waterproof bag where he had secured his phone and wallet. He heard the phone ringing, he held the bag close to his ear, yes, it was the special ringtone that indicated Meera's number. He unzipped the bag, and tilted it in such a way that water would not seep in, and turned the phone on speaker. Meera was worried; Kabeer had not even taken his car. Meera was calling from her car, she was coming to pick him up.

Kabeer immediately asked her to stop and go back, the place was far off, and she would have to cross the highway. It was risky to drive in such heavy rain and at the same time pointless; Kabeer had no intentions to come home until Saint was rescued. When Meera insisted upon, he scowled in anger and made it very clear that she should not come there, under any circumstances. He disconnected the phone and zipped the bag.

Kabeer looked towards the Saint. He was on the open ground, getting drenched in the rain. Kabeer could see the tears rolling from the Saints' eye; mingled with the rain just like his. The dog looked back at Kabeer and tried to clear the streaming rainwater from his eyes and ears with his paws. Kabeer looked around and saw that the umbrella, which was blown away by the gust of wind, was stuck under a tree. Kabeer picked-up it up and unfurled it again. He appreciated the villagers who had brought it in the first place. He moved towards the dog again with an open heart, expecting it to accept the protection of the umbrella. But unfortunately he was wrong. As soon as he tried to enter inside the circle, Saint left out a sound of warning. He tried to take another step, and the dog moved his body to get up. Kabeer immediately moved back out of the circle, and screamed loudly at the sky with a little anger, a little frustration and a loud cry of help – "MAHADEV…."

Kabeer held the open umbrella in an upright position and tried to stretch his arm as much as he could, but he could not get it closer to the dog. He looked around seeking something and found a long broken branch. By now the rain had increased, but lightning had stopped. Kabeer started to push the umbrella closer and closer towards the Saint with the help of the branch. He managed to move the umbrella inch by inch with the dog watching him without any repulsion. He felt relief when he saw the dog did not look repulsed by him. It was difficult to stay focused. The sharp rain shower blinded his eyes, making it difficult for him to stay focused, and suddenly the heavy rain and fast wind blew the umbrella again flew far towards the open road.

Kabeer ran after the umbrella, he slipped twice while doing so. His fall scraped his knee, and he began to bleed. Nevertheless, he managed to get hold of the umbrella. He walked back and tied a heavy stone to the umbrella handle, and finally placed it inside the marked circle. He pushed a big stone instead of the umbrella handle. This helped him, as the stone was big enough to be pushed with little focus, but at the same time being heavy, it required a bit more strength. He pushed it almost up to the

Saint; less than a foot away from him. The dog did not move at all, and he kept sitting in the rain trying to clear his eyes and ear from the pouring rainwater. Kabeer was aghast to realize that his huge effort had not at all resulted in helping the dog. Nothing seemed to be working, and this angered him, and when he looked at his scraped knee he got completely pissed off – it was bleeding profusely.

Kabeer pulled out his bandana from the bag. He placed his handkerchief on a big, clean leaf, and tied it around his wound. He looked at his water-drenched packet of cigarette and realized he could not have a smoke; thanks to Lord Indira, the rain God. Feeling helpless, he sat close to the boundary, with his legs crossed. He maintained a meditative pose and started chanting some *mantra*. Gradually he got deeply engrossed in the chanting and a sudden thunder, brought him back to the reality with a jitter. He opened his eyes and saw that the Saint was now trembling, and his tail was entirely down between the legs. A strong light was seen from the road, and he guessed that Meera must have come to pick him up. He looked towards the road. But, it was not Meera's car light that shone. It was a tree that had been struck with lightning and was burning to ashes.

Kabeer so much wanted to hug the scared dog, but alas, what could he do. He was now feeling tired, the rain was not showing any mercy, and neither was Saint. Kabeer lay down on the ground sideways, with his hand on his head to protect his face from the torrential downpour. He watched the dog silently, but with no thoughts running through his mind; lack of energy had numbed his mind. He could feel only sorrow. His mind could not even tell whether the sorrow was for the dog's suffering; the failed attempt to rescue; his own knee injury or everything put together.

However, his sorrow was short-lived. Saint moved under the shelter of the umbrella. Kabeer's tired red eyes allowed the first tear of warmth and joy stream down his cheek. At the same time, his numbed brain did not help to realize that this was the beginning of trust by the dog, for which he had been struggling since morning. He was not too tired to move, but lying down was actually restoring his energy. He had been so much involved for the entire day, both mentally and physically, that his physical fatigue had been completely ignored.

Kabeer kept staring at the dog and vice versa. Some more time passed like this, and once again, lightning struck. Though this was lighter than the one which had burnt the tree, it scared the dog thoroughly. He got uneasy; moved out of the umbrella; back in the rain. Kabeer cursed fate – DAMN MAN. The dog ran without direction inside the circle barking at the sky, but Kabeer remained still, a frown marred his brow.

Suddenly, Saint ran angrily towards Kabeer, as if Kabeer was responsible for the lightning. He stopped just in front of Kabeer's face. Kabeer could see the huge face of the giant, for a second he thought that his end has come. Saint had lost his sanity because of hunger, heat, snarling stray dogs and the rain. Any living being, after losing sanity, would and could do anything unpredictable. Saint unexpectedly yawned right in front of Kabeer's face. The cave of his mouth looked bigger than a wide-open mouth of a crocodile. Kabeer was sure that he would be swallowed any moment and sucked into this cave.

Things turned the other way, Saint moved back and walked towards the umbrella. From here, his limping was clearly visible. Kabeer guessed that some infection or lack of energy, or sheer exhaustion was the probable cause for Saint's limping. Now, instead of sitting under the umbrella, the Saint started pulling the rope with which the umbrella was tied to the stone.

The stone was huge, and it was a jaw-dropping scene to see a dog pulling such a heavy stone. Kabeer, without realizing got his energy back, and he sat back to watch. His mind also started to work, but not too smartly. He could not understand why the dog had developed so much hatred for the umbrella. What harm had the poor umbrella done? And then this lightning again struck – 'what the hell is with weather today?' Though during scorching summer this rain would have undoubtedly been a relief for many, but that moment for Kabeer and the dog, it was not helping at all. At least that's what Kabeer thought.

Saint again started to panic, and ran towards him, and started to bark at him. When Kabeer started to get up, the dog grabbed his shirt and started pulling. That was precisely what Faith used to do when he wanted to take Kabeer somewhere. He would pull him with his shirt towards the direction he would want Kabeer to go.

Kabeer moved in the direction Saint was pulling him. Saint brought Kabeer to the umbrella, let go off his shirt, sat under the umbrella and barked at Kabeer. Saint had left some space under the umbrella, Kabeer settled down to share the umbrella with the dog. He stretched out his leg, and the dog kept one of his forelegs on Kabeer's lap. This was exactly what Saint had done with the one-year-old kid (Pappu) when the kid's father wanted Pappu to come back.

Kabeer was startled, and tears started flowing from his eyes. This time his tears were not mixed with raindrops they were protected from rain by the umbrella. Kabeer placed his hand on the dog's head, and gave him a little rub; Saint didn't mind it. He then rubbed Saint's neck from the side, the dog dropped his head on Kabeer's lap and started to whine. Kabeer hugged the dog and burst out sobbing loudly. The dog too started to weep with loud howls. They both wept their hearts out.

By the time the tears of these two new friends dried up, the clouds also bid them goodbye and revealed a clear sky. Dawn had set in. Dawn was symbolic of Saint's new life. After facing the darkest night, the sun smiled brightly at him. The first thing that Kabeer wanted to do was to feed the dog, but he had nothing left with him. He had fed everything to the street dogs, but he did not repent that at all.

He called up Meera who attended the call in half ring. "Rescue successful" were the words he spoke, and he started to laugh with joy and pride. Meera too started to cry with tears of joy. "We are coming!" she exclaimed.

Kabeer questioned, "We? Who all are in this we?"

Meera replied, "Papa and Me."

Kabeer, "Why bother papa so early in the morning?"

Meera, "*Lallu*, me and papa had spent the entire night in the car near the highway waiting for your call. We are on the way, reaching in no time."

Kabeer, "But I need a lot of things, shall I message you?"

Meera, "We have got three huge bowls, water, dog food, glucose powder, milk, curd and *aloo ke parathe*. Now tell me what more you want."

Kabeer, "Cigarette."

Meera, "That's not possible. I am going to call off as we are almost there."

Kabeer's father was tense the whole night, and had got more stressed when Meera had started crying after hearing the words: "rescue successful". But maintaining his composure, he asked Meera if everything was OK? Meera, who treated her father-in-law as her own father, smiled and quizzed him as to how could he be such a good lawyer if he could not distinguish between tears of sorrow and the tears of joy.

Meera, "Yes, these are the tears of joy. The Saint is rescued..."

Papa exclaimed, "What? Are you serious? Oh, God .... Thanks a lot, God... Thanks a lot..." He raised his hand for a high five.

Meera clapped her hands with her father (-in-law) in a high five, and they both screamed loudly... "The Saint is rescued...."

THE SAINT WAS RESCUED!

The Saint and The Gang

Meera and Papa reached the place in their black WagonR with a dickey full of stuff. Kabeer had dropped two sentences of two words each to two persons – "Saint Rescued. Call Back." This was to Pratima and Dr Divya.

Meera saw the scene from inside the car. She saw that the Saint was asleep on Kabeer's lap in a carefree manner. As the car drew near, the dog lifted his head but continued to have both his forelegs on Kabeer's lap. She quickly switched on the phone camera's video recording button, and she stepped out of the car, recording everything. She was followed by Papa, with the bag of food in one hand, and the bowls in the other hand. Meera had seen many videos of Saint, but seeing him live in his huge size was altogether a different experience, especially the way he was on Kabeer's lap like a grown-up baby. Papa, too was stunned at the size of the dog but had his wits intact.

"Oh, holy cow! What kind of a dog is this? How can somebody abandon such a beautiful creature of God? See Papa how lovely they both look together..." Meera exclaimed.

Papa replied, "I told you before you married Kabeer that he is a complete dog, at least he is now in good company. Company of the type of creatures from his likes." Both of them burst into laughter.

Then the recording was disturbed by a phone call on Meera's number. She immediately took the call, and spoke those unbelievable magic words in the phone – "Rescue Successful!"

It was Dr Divya on the other side, and with equal joy, she responded, "I know, I got Kabeer's message. I am trying his number but not able to connect."

Meera, "Battery might have dried out. He is right here, you wanna speak to him?"

Dr Divya, "Just give him a message I am on my way and would be there very soon. And one more thing Meera, Except liquids, do not serve anything to Saint yet."

Meera, "Sure."

Meanwhile, Pratima's call was on waiting mode as Meera was speaking to Dr Divya. Meera called Pratima back. She knew that Pratima must also be aware of the successful rescue. After the joyous sharing of the news, Meera walked towards Kabeer to hand over the phone to him, and that is when the Saint suddenly barked loud, in a slightly offensive manner.

Kabeer immediately rubbed the dog's head which helped to relax him. Kabeer took the phone from Meera and signaled her to maintain some distance from them. After offering his thanks to God, Kabeer told Pratima to go to his home, and take Faith for a walk, as his mother was unwell to take Faith. Kabeer's mother suffered from a knee joint problem. Apart from the family, Faith was comfortable only with Dr Divya, Pratima and Shivani. Only these three ladies could take him out for a walk. Pratima was more than glad to take Faith for a walk because both of them enjoyed the run. Unlike Kabeer, she did not just take Faith for a short walk and then sit-back to play the fetch game. Pratima would run with Faith till they both would pant in complete exhaustion.

Meera made glucose water for Saint in a bowl, and for Kabeer in a glass. She sat down with Papa on the ground and started discussing the rescue. Kabeer disclosed in bits and pieces but promised to tell everything in detail at home over a cup of hot coffee. He was still very observant and cautious about the dog. Kabeer now wanted to pee; as he got up to walk towards the trees, Saint stopped drinking his glucose water, and ran towards Kabeer, and held him by his shirt, and started to whine softly. Kabeer immediately sat down on his knees, and hugged the dog and said that he would never leave him and he could trust him. Kabeer then took the dog along towards the trees. As Kabeer started to pee, the Saint also went to the nearby tree and peed. Kabeer looked at the dog and smiled broadly. The dog too looked back at Kabeer and matched his smile. When they started their walk back, Papa looked at them with affection, and then spat thrice on the floor in a systematic manner. This was a belief of protecting someone from people's evil eyes, especially at the time of being appreciated.

Sun had brightened the day, and Dr Divya came in her Scorpio. Saint immediately got alert, looked at the Scorpio, and his tail started to wag, but as soon as Dr Divya came out of the Scorpio, the Saint drew back in a not-so-excited state of mind. The dog was completely at ease, he had finally trusted Kabeer. But his trust did not extend to all those whom Kabeer trusted, that included the doctor also, and it was about to become a problem for his checkup. Divya being a doctor, was fully aware that Saint would not be as easy as other patients. Saint had just been rescued and was still trying to comprehend his rescuc.

Dr Divya took baby steps, literally, towards the dog. She wore a pair of tight jeans and half-sleeve kurta. While she was closing in, Saint expressed his discomfort with a soft growl, and then looked at Kabeer. While Kabeer rubbed his head to relax him, Dr Divya stepped back to let the comfortable distance between her and Saint. Kabeer shared with her, "Every time he sees your car, there is a happy wag in his tail, but as soon as you step down he sulks back. Why?"

"His previous master must have been the owner of a Scorpio or a similar-looking SUV." Dr Divya knew dogs well.

She also told Kabeer to start talking to Saint in a human language. She estimated that the dog was approximately four to five years old, and he must have learnt some human words as commands; especially the basic commands like 'go', 'no', 'stop', 'come', etc. He would also know other words used in daily life, such as '*khaana*' or meal, '*sona*' or sleep, and should be responsive to nicknames like *babu*, *guddu* etc. As of now, Saint was responding to the body language, and not words. Saint was comfortable and responsive, and that was more than enough.

Dr Divya looked at Saint from a distance and immediately made a note of things which called for immediate attention. Saint was suffering from a skin infection, evidently, and for sure would have been infested with ticks too. She was scared if Saint had maggots too. At some places little patches were apparent and seemed to be like wounds. But that could only be confirmed after his fur was trimmed or shaved.

She confidently sat close to Saint without showing any signs of hesitation. The dog looked blankly at Kabeer, and Kabeer rubbed his head, repeating the words, "Doctor, *beta*. Doctor." Probably Saint understood the word 'Doctor' and responded positively. He was turned upside down for a thorough examination. Good News–Saint, was cooperating, bad news–he had suffered sunburns.

Now the doctor rubbed her hand all over the dog and asked Kabeer to take the dog to her clinic in her car. That seemed to be a good idea as a Scorpio had always made him wag his tail. Though Kabeer hesitated a bit as he felt that a Scorpio would make Saint recall his home, then he thought that Saint anyway could never forget his old home where he had spent a major part of his life. And the fact that he had been adamant about being with his old master only, clearly established the fact that he was very happy in his old home.

Kabeer took his bag of clothes from Meera, and changed his clothes behind the trees, and walked back. Yes, Saint was with him throughout this exercise. While the dog walked along with Kabeer behind the trees, Dr Divya noticed the limp in his walk. She crossed her finger and murmured a prayer. She knew that something was wrong with the dog. She prayed that what she feared should not turn out to be true.

Kabeer was now in a grey track pant with a white t-shirt with a cute picture of a puppy printed on it saying, "I don't mind who dies in a movie as long as the dog lives." Kabeer and the doctor along with Saint drove in her Scorpio, while Meera and Papa went back home, and later Meera went ahead with her office schedule. Pratima too left from Kabeer's home for the clinic.

After the dog was bathed entirely and his sunburns were treated, his infections were closely monitored. The doctor was a little relieved, as they were not severe. However, to be on the safer side they decided to completely shave his fur so that limited eczema does not spread underneath the thick coat of hair. A shave made Saint look comparatively smaller but cleaner, his ears were cleaned thoroughly, and ticks were plucked from his body using a special tweezer.

It was then when Dr Divya spilled the beans, "He is limping severely, and I fear something serious but won't comment until I am sure about it. We will have to get an X-ray done."

The dog had to be under anesthesia to get his legs straight for the X-Ray. She called up a laboratory and fixed an immediate appointment. There was still one hour for her clinic to start, so Dr Divya accompanied them. With modern technology, the report was ready in a jiffy. Unfortunately, her fear turned true; Saint was suffering from Hip Dysplasia.

{Hip Dysplasia is a disease where the hip joints are not correctly positioned. There is a gap between the holder's bone at the hip; and the bulb of the bone in the dog's leg. This dysplasia was unfortunately in Saint's both the legs. Dysplasia has no cure, except a surgery, where metal plates and sockets are placed, but even then, the success ratio usually is less than 10%. Only selected-few doctors do these operations. Since the bones are not positioned correctly they rub depreciatingly while walking, and deterioration leads to arthritis in old age.}

Dr Divya advised Kabeer not to lose hope, as it was not a deadly disease, and dogs never die because of hip dysplasia. She assured him that she would consult her senior, and find out ways to ensure that Saint lived a happy and active life despite this ailment.

Now the next big question was parenting the dog. Saint faced a lot of difficulties while placing his trust on Kabeer, and so keeping him with Shivani (who was ever ready to foster a dog till it got a permanent home) was totally wiped out. Kabeer and Saint were two souls made for each other but Faith, Kabeer's possessive buddy, would not accept Saint at all, especially a dog much bigger than himself; Saint was almost five times Faith's weight.

Kabeer planned to introduce Faith and Saint in the garden of his apartment block, and then take Saint to his home. However, that could happen only in the evening as the weather was too hot to keep anyone in the open garden.

Kabeer, Pratima and the Saint were now in Pratima's car. Kabeer was sitting in the backseat with the dog. She was more worried about parenting the dog. After almost 15 minutes of silence, Kabeer said that he would take the dog home directly, and see what happens. He had to keep his faith in Faith, and fear nothing, 'fear is faith in the wrong place'. Pratima asked him twice if he was sure of what he wanted to do. Kabeer nodded.

Pratima drove towards Kabeer's home, and during the entire journey, Kabeer kept rubbing the beads of his *rudraksha mala*, hung around his neck. On the way, they had halted to get some bricks of ice-cream. They reached their block, and Pratima drove the car into the basement parking lot. As per the rules of their apartment block, only residents were allowed to park there, but Pratima and her good deeds had made her like a resident of the society. She was allowed to enjoy all the benefits which only society residents were allowed to. From the basement they took the lift to ninth floor of the twelve storey building. Just beside the lift was Kabeer's home.

Kabeer rang the doorbell, and Papa came to open the door. There were two doors in the panel, one was completely opaque made of pure teak-wood, while the other one had aluminum rods put in symmetry in the wooden frame of the door. Opaque door was generally left open as it allowed air circulation. Other two purposes it served, was to see the guests and visitors and obstruct Faith from rushing on everyone at their door.

Saint was standing outside with Kabeer and Pratima when Faith came running to the door. It was impossible to contain Faith's excitement whenever anybody from the family came back home. Now Kabeer and Pratima were family, and they had come back along with a guest, another dog. Faith was thrilled to see Kabeer; he brought his forelegs up on the aluminum rods, then ran back in the hall and again rushed back to the door. The first sigh of relief was that Saint was not bugged by the presence of Faith; he was just looking at the other dog curiously. His head would tilt right and then lift in amusement just observing the other dog's antics. Finally, the trio entered, and Faith placed his forelegs on Kabeer's chest trying to lick his face. Faith welcomed Pratima in the same manner, and then stood in front of Saint, hardly two feet away.

There was an extreme silence among the six beings – Mummy, Papa, Faith, Saint, Kabeer and Pratima. Faith had never seen such a dog; he was curious and started smelling the new four-legged visitor. Saint had seen many street dogs and Labradors since Faith was a mix Labrador, his appearance was no novelty for Saint. Faith smelled the sunburnt area of Saint, on the side rib where betadine was applied. Faith smelled the betadine and recognized it immediately; few times Faith had also been treated with the same.

Faith very well knew for what purpose it was used. Betadine was applied in quite a few places on Saint's body, within no time Faith understood that the new guest was injured. Faith touched his nose on Saint's nose, their teeth were very close, and Kabeer and Papa were prepared for any aggression by any of the two.

Faith after smelling Saint's nose licked it, Saint too did the same. Faith's tail started the wagging action and that too in a very rapid motion. Faith communicated something in a very soft bark. Saint either didn't understand or chose not to reply. Faith moved few steps back, and Saint stood-up from his sitting position. Faith again made some sounds, but Saint responded only by a confused left and right tilting of his head. It was clear that Saint could not understand the verbal language of Faith.

Faith came forward, held Saint's ear in his teeth and pulled it. Saint jerked a little to free his ear, but Faith pulled the ear a little more before leaving it and moved a couple of steps back. This time Saint got his message and moved towards Faith. Faith started moving inside the hall with his eyes fixed at Saint. Saint followed him, and everyone followed the duo. It seemed to be the beginning of a new friendship; and an essential one.

Faith escorted Saint first to the kitchen that was on the left-hand side of the large hall. He placed his front foot on the kitchen slab and kept pointing towards the things on the slab with some instruction in low barks. Saint quietly followed, because of his size he was not required to jump to see the things on the kitchen counter. Faith then came out of the kitchen, and crossed the hall to reach the balcony, adjacent to the hall; Saint quietly followed.

In the balcony, there was a flower bed full of various plants, and two special ones – a rose and a *tulsi*. Faith leaned towards the rose plant, smelled the biggest rose, and moved back, allowing space for Saint to follow suit. Saint copied Faith but kept on smelling the biggest rose for a long while before turning around with a broad smile. Faith too was all smiles, and then Saint turned back to the plant and started smelling all the roses of the plant; Saint was in love with roses.

Faith turned around, everyone was observing the duo with moist eyes and sloppy smiles. Faith jumped with his forelegs on Kabeer with a swift wag of his tail and gave few overwhelming licks to his master before turning back to Saint. Faith now nibbled Saint to draw his attention away from the rose plant.

Though Saint was apprehensive to part with roses, at the same time he was curious to experience more of what Faith had to offer. Faith moved towards the *tulsi* plant, couple of leaves had dropped on to the floor. He picked one of the leaves with his tongue, exhibited the *tulsi* leaf on his tongue and gulped it. This surprised everyone; Meera had this habit of plucking few *tulsi* leaves every morning and giving it to everyone including Faith. When Meera had offered the leaf for the first time to

Faith, he had liked it so much that he actually ran towards the *tulsi* plant to pluck few leaves on his own. A firm 'NO' from Meera had stopped him from the act, and to also ensure that he was not supposed to touch the plant. However none knew that he kept checking for the fallen leaves, and ate whenever he found any. Saint also picked the second fallen leaf, showed his tongue to Faith and gulped it. Their bond was getting deeper.

Faith then took his guest to the smallest room, which actually was his room though he was rarely found there. The room also accommodated an eight hundred litre water tank in a corner with two rescued turtles – Shubh and Labh (exotic species, permitted by law to be kept as pets). Diagonally opposite to the tank was a single bed covered with a bedsheet with pictures of cute puppies and a bone-shaped pillow. Near the foot of the bed, there was a short stand with two big bowls, one was filled with water, and the other was empty. Faith drank water from the water bowl and then invited his guest to have some water. The Saint drank all the water and dirtied the bowl with his ever-flowing saliva. Faith looked at the bowl and then at Kabeer, he had an unpleasant expression.

Faith again looked inside the bowl and then barked at Kabeer. He did not like the saliva mixed water. Mummy went into the kitchen and filled the other empty bowl with fresh water, which then Faith gulped a little. The Saint was following Faith's every move, and therefore he went near this other bowl too. But before he could dip his tongue into the bowl, Faith barked loudly and stopped him. Saint looked quizzingly at Faith; this was the first time that he was stopped from doing something by Faith. He then tried to drink water from the previous bowl, and Faith did not react to that. Saint understood that the water bowls were assigned.

Kabeer noticed when Saint was drinking a lot of water had spilled on the floor because of his flabby mouth; he made a mental note of finding a solution for the same, and also to buy new bowls for their food. Kabeer also realized that Saint's bowl ought to be lifted higher, as he had to almost kneel to drink the water. Faith now took Saint into a small bathroom, and peed near the drain and came out, Saint did the same. Kabeer recalled how difficult it was to make Faith understand that in case of emergency, he could use the drain in the bathroom, and now Faith had explained everything to the new dog with such ease.

Faith took Saint to the parent's room, moved around, and then came out to get into Kabeer and Meera's room. As soon as Faith entered this room, he immediately jumped on to the bed and ran up and down the king-size mattress. Saint didn't do that, he just moved around, and then sat by the side of the bed. Faith jumped down from the bed, and picked a ball from the corner, behind the door, and again jumped on to the bed. Faith was tempting Saint with the ball, but Saint kept looking at him and the ball with his hanging tongue.

Faith dropped the ball near Saint's mouth and waited. As soon as Saint tried to pick the ball Faith grabbed it, and jumped again on the bed. This was enough for Faith to encourage him, and he too jumped on to the bed, but could not make it in one single jump. He climbed on the bed like a stair and moved towards Faith, who then ran out of the room with the ball. Saint too ran behind him while slipping on the way and everybody followed to see them. By now Kabeer had made a third mental note; he will have to do something to prevent Saint's slipping, probably a carpet.

Faith ran into the hall jumping on to the sofa and ran helter-skelter, and this time Saint too was a party to it. They were now friends and playing, everybody was joyous. Mummy started the preparations for lunch, and Pratima made some *sharbat* for everyone. By the time everyone settled down, even Faith and his new friend were tired of playing and had laid down in front of the cooler in the hall, for a nap.

After having *sharbat* Kabeer went for a shower and changed into *kurta pajama* to join everybody for lunch. During lunch, he narrated the entire story of the dog's rescue in great detail. After lunch, Pratima left for her home, and everybody in the Kapoor family retired for the noon sleep. Faith joined Papa in his room, and the Saint went to Kabeer's room. Kabeer and the Saint slept like never before in the cool air-conditioned room, and it was around 8:00pm when they both finally woke up. Kabeer and Papa took both the dogs out for their small evening walk, discussing finance and other matters. Meanwhile, Dr Divya called to inform that she was coming home with the details of Saint's treatment.

Dr Divya and Meera met each other in the lift coincidentally, and both arrived home together. Faith was mad like always and jumped all over them. Though Saint came near the door but sat calmly. The doctor then patted Saint's head, and he wagged his tail lightly; he actually didn't like doctors much. But when Meera tried to rub the Saint's head, he jerked his head off and barked at her. Kabeer immediately came forward and relaxed him. He told Meera that it's his first day and he would take some time to get comfortable with her. But Saint and Faith had developed a strong bond, and had been together all the time except when they had gone to sleep; Saint didn't leave Kabeer for anyone.

Meera and Dr Divya were surprisingly happy to see the video of Faith giving a house tour to his new friend, also the quite surprising episode of the *tulsi* leaves. It made their jaws drop in an amazed "awwww".

Now Dr Divya initiated the discussion for which she had come: treating the dog's hip dysplasia. The doctor said, "Dysplasia is a term used for all kind of joint displacements like hip dysplasia, knee dysplasia, and shoulder dysplasia etc. These are common with large breed dogs like German Shepherd, Rottweiler, even retrievers (Labrador Retrievers and Golden Retrievers) and sometimes even with small breeds like Lhasa and Pug also. The problem becomes severe only with large dogs, because of their huge weight. The heavier the weight, the more pressure is put on the joints, and the condition worsens. Now coming to our baby, the Saint is not just a large breed, but a giant breed dog, like Great Dane and Mastiffs. There is a course of five injections, that has to be administered for five weeks, but the most important thing is to get his muscles holding the hip joint stronger somehow. Exercise is the only way, though some steroids can also be given for making the muscles strong. However, the side-effects are something which I am not comfortable with. I would, therefore, avoid steroids."

Kabeer replied, "I can take him for long walks, jogging and play those running games. Apart from that if there is any particular exercise to be done, just say so."

The doctor countered, "No, Kabeer it is rather the other way, he should not be running at all for a long time. Never. Look, whenever he stands or walks his entire body puts pressure on his joints. The more he walks or runs, the more pressure will be on the joints. The bones will then rub against each other, which would further exacerbate the condition. First of all, you need to get the house covered with carpet, where ever he plays. The surface should be padded to reduce the impact on his joints. Secondly, this floor is too slippery, and any major slip while running may hurt him badly. So, this carpeting will be good for Faith also. Saint should be walked at least twice a day at a slow pace for 25 to 30 minutes, preferably on soft surface like a garden."

Meera asked, "Doctor, will that be enough exercise to strengthen the muscles?"

Dr Divya replied, "No Meera, not at all. He needs leg exercise of hours every day, with good protein meal."

Mummy then asked, "But if he does not run or jump, then how will his legs be exercised? It's like two contradictory things to be done at the same time. To strengthen the leg muscle, leg exercises are required, but all the leg exercises will put pressure on the joints. What's the solution then?" Mummy looked upset and turned to look at everybody for an answer.

Saint was lying on the floor, chewing the ball, and completely ignoring the discussion. And Faith was sitting on the sofa with Papa, and he had his forelegs on Papa's lap. Papa proposed, "Swimming?"

Dr Divya, "BINGO Sir. Swimming is the only magical exercise where leg muscles are worked out, but there is no pressure on the joints. But where will you get him to swim? There are no commercial swimming pools for dogs in Ahmedabad. And even if you work out in somebody's farmhouse, it could be for a day every week. But, Saint requires it daily; that too for at least two to three hours every day."

Kabeer, "That shouldn't be much of a task. We will get something done. But it would take some time. Anything I should know about the water? Anything specific?"

Dr Divya, "Nothing about the water except, of course, that it has to be clean. Saint Bernards are not very immune to skin infections, especially when they are not in their own natural habitat. He can start his swimming only after a week, as he requires that much time to get completely cured of his infections. But, tell me what's on your mind."

Kabeer then replied, "How about a lake or a pond? I know a pond in the interiors of *Bopal.*"

Dr Divya, "I know that pond, but it will not do. Cattle bathe in that pond, and the water will be surely infectious for Saint. Lake would do, but again do we have a clean lake in Ahmedabad? "

Kabeer said, "How about *Sabarmati*?"

Dr Divya replied, "Only in the middle of the river. The sides are not very clean. And, before taking him to the centre of the river, we need to check if he knows swimming, or this will be his first time."

Kabeer, "I will try to get some farmhouse on rent for a week or so. And then we can take him to the river."

Dr Divya, "That sounds good to me. But before he begins his swimming, I will check for the infections and open wounds to be completely cured. I would also like to observe his swimming in the pool. OK?"

Meera said, "Hey Doc, you sound like a school principal. Why don't we have a small get together on the last day in the farmhouse? A get together of all the dogs we know around? You will be allowed only with your Rocky, or else no entry." Then Meera mimicked Dr Divya and said "OK?" and everybody broke into laughter. By now, Pratima had also entered the room; she had missed a major part of the discussion. Sensing the cheer, she suggested taking a picture of all of them together.

Meera brought her semi-professional Canon camera with the tripod stand. Everybody gathered against the wall, which had a 3D wallpaper of wild bamboos. Everyone was ready to be clicked. The camera was put on a 10 seconds timer for an auto-click, and it clicked it perfectly. Everybody had sat on their knees, Mummy and Papa had taken left and right side respectively. Mummy had Dr Divya to her right, and Dr Divya had Meera to her right. Papa had Pratima to his left, and Pratima had Kabeer to her left. Kabeer and Meera were in the centre with Saint and Faith in front of them. They knelt on the floor with their heads held up. This picture was a reflection of Saint's new life, new family, and new friends. This was a new Gang. Indeed he was the only 'Saint' (even in his nature) in the Gang; The Saint of the Gang.

The Saint and the Gang!!!

Saint - The Stalwart

Saint and Kabeer were still carrying their sleep debt. Post dinner with little discussion about the arrangement for a swimming pool, everyone retired for the day, except Meera and Kabeer. Kabeer narrated the entire rescue story to Meera with a lot of descriptions and gesticulations. At times, he was repetitive about what he had done and mimicked what Saint did. Meanwhile, Saint was lying down near the bed but was not asleep. He was listening to the story as if it was someone else's rescue story. Kabeer almost reconstructed the entire rescue scene before Meera, and as a reward he got a very passionate kiss from Meera which ended after few minutes. While they were kissing, Saint had turned his head the other way and dozed-off. Actually, the kiss was broken by Saint's snoring. This made the startled couple to break into laughter. The dog snored quite loudly like a typical old villager. Meera and Kabeer switched-off the light, hugged each other, and again started to kiss each other, which was followed by passionate and intrinsic lovemaking.

Next morning again it was Faith, the wake-up alarm, who at 6:00 am woke up Kabeer and Saint. Meera had already started her day with boiling the milk and making herself some green tea. After freshening-up Meera and Kabeer, both went down with Faith and Saint for the morning walk. They discussed the arrangement of the swimming pool. Kabeer himself was a great swimmer and knew two swimming classes in Ahmedabad. However, the couple had their doubts about these swimming classes being of any help to Saint.

A ray of hope was Pratima. Her father owned a beautiful farmhouse with a large swimming pool. They both had been there for a lot of parties, but Pratima's father was not a dog lover. In fact, he was a dog hater, though he had never hurt any dog. His hatred was only because of Pratima's over-involvement with dogs, and that too stray dogs that roamed on the streets. Meera also knew a few people who owned farmhouses and promised that she would speak to them. She did not know if anything would come out of it. After the walk, both of them sat down on a bench in the garden of their apartment block and started the 'fetch-the-ball' game. It was more fun than usual, as this time Faith and Saint competed with each other to fetch the ball. The day had started with immense energy.

Later that day, it was around 2:00 pm in the afternoon. And the answer from every one of their friends and circle, who had a farmhouse with a swimming pool, was negative. The only good news of the day was that a two-year-old female golden retriever named Coffee which had been rescued by the gang, and fostered by Shivani was now adopted. A family in the *Vastrapur* area of Ahmedabad had adopted her. The family was already parenting a female Labrador retriever called *Pari* (fairy). So the family had been looking for a companion for Pari for the past two months, as their daughter had got married, and left for foreign shores. They wanted to adopt a dog and not buy, and by the grace of God the dots were connected for both *Pari* and Coffee.

In the morning, Saint was not allowing Kabeer to leave him alone, but then Faith handled the situation with the help of some calcium bones given by Papa.

Meera and Kabeer had invited Pratima and Shivani for a lunch celebration to celebrate Coffee's happiness. Shivani kept insisting, "Availability of a swimming pool for the dog is not a big challenge, all we need to do is think out of the box. It just seems as impossible as his rescue was, all those who tried the conventional and time tested ways failed because they all had missed the basic point of winning the trust of the dog in a rescue. Once his trust was won, the rescue was a cakewalk.

Similarly, we need to work on basic points to arrange the pool, and it will surely work out."

Meera agreed with Shivani, and they tried to zero-in the task in hand, once again.

Meera, "The very first point is that the swimming pool to be availed for Saint has to be a private swimming pool and not a commercial one. Hotels and swimming institutes will not allow them as this would stop their commercial activity. Secondly, the dog has just recovered from the skin infection, and this would also be a point to worry about for the commercial owners."

Pratima said, "So true. If somebody comes to know that a rescued dog with skin infection has bathed in the pool, then nobody will pay to use that particular swimming pool."

Meera said, "So. We need a person who either owns a swimming pool or knows the owner of a private swimming pool."

Kabeer, "In short, we need a resourceful person."

Meera, "A resourceful person, and the person should be a DOG LOVER too."

Pratima replied, "So true. My dad is also very resourceful, but..."

Kabeer said, "Not only your dad *yaar*. Since morning we have approached so many resourceful people, but all have denied access just for one reason – Dog. They are not dog lovers, and those who are dog lovers do not have the required resource."

Pratima, "Does that mean we are again back to square one?"

Shivani said, "No, dear. Till now we were looking for a swimming pool, which is the end result. Now, we know the way, we need to look for a resourceful dog lover."

Kabeer, "Builders?"

Meera, "Are they dog Lovers? Please Kabeer, let your mind think. Now don't say that your thinking is coming up with such answers. Relax your mind and think hard. Just think."

Kabeer, "A cigarette would help me to…"

Meera abruptly interrupted Kabeer with a big frown, "Then Don't think." And after a pause, "Just eat…"

Pratima said, "Dog shops?"

Shivani said, "Dog hostels?"

And then the waiter came in and enquired, "Shall I serve the pizza?"

Meera ignoring the waiter exclaimed, "IDIOTS…!!" The waiter was taken aback; he did not realize it was not him that the lady was referring to. Meera continued, "NGOs… NGOs. Damn it, NGOs." Once the waiter realized that the word was not meant for him, he quietly served the pizza slices to everyone.

Shivani joined in excitedly, "Bingo. Yes, NGOs are resourceful, and of course dog lovers. Meera, you are a darling. Muaah…"

Meera pulled the collar of her *kurta* up in her own appreciation. Kabeer patted her back. It was not at all difficult to get a list of NGOs in Ahmedabad. A lot of them had tried to rescue Saint, and they were in the news too. Kabeer then said that it would be best to reach out to those NGOs that had attempted to rescue Saint, as they already know and feel for him.

Till then, Pratima had started the online search and was noting down the names of the NGOs and their numbers on a tissue paper. She managed to list out seven in all. Kabeer took a bite of the pizza, and announced, "First thing I would do tomorrow is to contact each of these NGO. Meanwhile, Pratima you should continue your search for NGOs."

Meera stared at Kabeer with squinting eyes and said, "Kabeer, you are a lazy bum. You know what? If you want something from someone you don't even know then you are actually asking it from the universe and not the person: the universal energy a.k.a (also known as) God. If you ask with great earnestness, whatever you want, you get it. The universe gives speedily, and never delays, but you are doing it.

Kabeer, "What am I doing to cause a delay?"

Meera, "May I know what important thing you have to do now that you are postponing your task till tomorrow? Are you procrastinating? Remember the thing you delay for no reason is the thing you should do in the same moment itself, just as you are stuffing the pizza in your mouth now." Meera looked at the girls, and pointed towards Kabeer, "Look at him, does he even look worried about Saint? All he is bothered about is the cheesy pizza. My dear husband, Saint's rescue is not the end of the task; the task has just begun. So you, better start calling NGOs now."

Kabeer had had more than the share of his lecture for the day than he had his share of the pizza. He asked in a shocked manner, "Shall I start calling them from here itself? While eating?"

Meera replied firmly, "Yes."

Kabeer groaned, "Oh God… Someone, please rescue me too… Pratima give me the list." Saying this Kabeer extended his hand, and took the list of the NGOs from her and dialed the first number on the list.

"Hi, I wanted to speak to the rescue team. {A little pause while the person on the other side spoke} Yes, it's regarding a rescue. {Another pause} No, this is urgent, maybe by the time team decides to respond, it could be too late. If a senior person could help me over the phone, it would be of great help. {a small pause} That's awesome. {Another pause} Yeah, yeah, I will hold the line." Kabeer covered the phone with his hand and shared that the team had gone for a rescue, but the Chairperson of the Trust is available, and the receptionist had informed that she would check if he is free to talk to him. Meera replied, "Hmmm… What did I…" But before she could complete her sentence Kabeer was back on the phone.

He continued, "Hello Sir, I am Kabeer, a dog lover, and with the help of some of my friends, I try to rescue dogs. {Pause} Sir if you remember a few days back your team tried to rescue a Saint Bernard, which was stranded near the highway and was not allowing anybody to come near him. {Pause} Sir, we have been able to rescue him, and he is now at my home. {Pause} That's a long story, sir, I will tell you once we meet, but right now there is something very important that we need for Saint. I mean the same Saint Bernard, we have named him Saint. {Pause} Sir, he has been diagnosed with Hip Dysplasia, and as per the doctor, swimming will be very helpful for his recovery. We will be taking him to the river for his swim, but initially for few practice sessions, we need a swimming pool for a week. {Pause} Don't worry sir; I am a state-level swimmer. {Pause} Oh, that would be great. {Pause} No, no, no issues sir. He is recovering from some skin infection and would be able to swim only after a week's time. {A long Pause} Sure sir, yes my number is **********. Thanks a lot sir thanks a lot. {Pause} sure, sure."

The girls in the gang were looking at Kabeer and his broad smile with anxiety. Meera felt he looked like a real mad man, with his amoeba-shaped beard, his overgrown hair, and his nicotine-stained teeth bracketed by a weird smile. Kabeer looked at the sky and opened his arms in the air, and shouted loudly, forgetting that they were in a public place – MAHADEV, MAHADEV!!! Everybody in the restaurant looked at him. However, he ignored them all and looked at the girls sitting with him and said, "Guess What?" And there, a tone in his phone indicated that a message had been received.

All three girls chorused, "What?"

Kabeer smiled and replied, "The Chairperson is an NRI, and has his own farmhouse located in *Guma* (name of a place hardly 10 km from Kabeer's residence). He is leaving for US tomorrow night, and has agreed to give the keys of his farmhouse to us, to use his swimming pool for Saint."

Pratima and Shivani did a high five, and Meera said, "What did I tell you? The universe helps only if you don't delay. Now what more proof do you want? Anyway, I feel there is surely something more you have to share, no one parts with keys to their farmhouse to a stranger, just because of a story told over the phone."

Kabeer concurred with her, "Yes, you are right. He wants to see Saint, and the doctor treating him. And there will be a security guard in the farmhouse who would keep a check on what we do there." He pointed to his phone and, "He has messaged me his number, and his address from where I should pick him. So, who's gonna join me?"

Shivani suggested, "Meera, it will be great if you could go. Anyways the entire credit of getting this swimming pool goes to you only. You came up with the inspiration, you zeroed in on our requirement. It was also originally your idea to approach NGOs, and it was you who pushed Kabeer to call right now. What say, Pratima?"

Pratima agreed, "Yes, Only if Meera doesn't have any prior engagement."

Meera was a person loved by this entire group of dog Lovers. She was a corporate lady in a senior position but was always available in times of need. She had never tried to show-off, though she was extremely intelligent. To everyone's joy and surprise she agreed to accompany Kabeer, though she had an important meeting lined-up. However, she thought she could manage that later. After finishing the lunch, Meera paid the bill and told Kabeer that she would be free in two hours, and then they could go.

Pratima and Shivani had come in the same car. So Shivani took the keys of Kabeer's car to be left at his residence. It was decided that from there Pratima would drive Shivani from Kabeer's home to her destination. Kabeer dropped Meera at her office and went to meet his ex-colleagues.

Later Meera and Kabeer drove to the address that was messaged to them and called-up Mihir Mehta (the chairperson of the NGO) once they reached his place. Mihir insisted that they stepped in to have some coffee before leaving. It was a big bungalow and was located in the poshest area of Ahmedabad,

Satellite Road. There was a Jaguar parked inside the gate, and just beside it was the stone path leading towards the home. On the other side of this path was a garden, with trees along the boundary wall. The flowers on the tree were adorning the wall. Mihir was sitting in the garden, though it was summers. Still, it was pleasant as the sun was setting, and its rays filtered through the trees around them.

Mihir was a young man about the same age as Kabeer, though he looked younger than Kabeer. He shook hands with the couple and instructed his servant to serve water and coffee. Kabeer and Meera kept addressing him as Sir, to which he objected and insisted that they call him by his first name.

By the time water, coffee and snacks were served; Kabeer had briefly narrated the rescue story followed by the doctor's diagnosis and the treatment. He did not give a detailed narration the way he had given to Meera. He did not want to waste time. Mihir was very happy to hear about the story, and he confessed that he had some doubts if that call was a genuine one or a fake. Now, after having met them, and learning that Saint was being treated by Dr Divya, his doubts had vanished. However, he still wanted to see Saint and meet the doctor too.

Kabeer excused for a moment and informed Dr Divya about Mihir, his wish to meet her, and the reason for it. After finishing the coffee they left the venue. While Kabeer and Meera left in their car, Mihir drove his own car. Upon Dr Divya's insistence, they headed first to her clinic.

Dr Divya met Mihir and briefed him about Saint's current condition and prescribed treatment. She also added how Saint was still coming to terms with his abandonment, and hence was not so friendly with new faces. Kabeer was still the face he actually fully trusted and to some extent Faith. Apart from these two beings, everyone else was yet to be emotionally close. She also appreciated Faith for being such a great friend of Saint's. It was a boon; else it would have not been possible for Kabeer to go even to the loo alone. Kabeer agreed with her and shared that it had actually happened at the rescue spot.

Everybody laughed over it, but Dr Divya did not lose the seriousness on her face. She continued to list out the challenges that Kabeer and Saint had to face, "Hip Dysplasia takes a very serious turn when the dog is old, roughly around 8 years of age. Moreover, if the precaution is not taken now, then it could also be fatal."

It was actually good that Mihir had managed to meet the doctor, as no one else would have been able to explain the situation in such detail that Mihir understood the urgent requirement for a swimming pool.

After the meeting, Mihir and Dr Divya shook hands firmly and thanked each other from the bottom of their heart for everything they were doing or would be doing for Saint. Dr Divya was so worried that her eyes had gone moist a couple of times, only her professionalism held the tears back. Moreover, she was a doctor who has been practicing since last 7/8 years, and if now she had got so emotional, then it was surely because Saint meant a lot to her.

Now Kabeer, Meera and Mihir together had reached his home, the main wooden door was open, and the door with grills was shut. Kabeer rang the doorbell, Faith and Saint both came running to the door; Papa opened the door and welcomed them in. Faith started to jump on Kabeer and Meera, later both the dogs smelled Mihir from his toe to his waist and after that only allowed him in. It is believed that a dog can judge the intention of a person by smelling his feet.

Saint was still apprehensive about Mihir's presence. He had taken a seat far from the door and started continuously barking, angrily at Mihir. Kabeer quickly went to Saint and hugged him warmly. The dog put his forelegs on Kabeer's shoulder and started to lick him eagerly. Saint had been away from Kabeer for the whole day, and now he didn't want Kabeer to stay far. He slathered saliva all over Kabeer's face. Kabeer was treated to a great facial by Saint. Kabeer sat down on the floor with Saint, and Faith too joined them.

It did not require any analysis or great observation to understand the relationship of Kabeer and his dogs. Mihir had been a witness to Saint when he was abandoned, and he was seeing Saint in a completely different emotional state. Mihir's eyes were moist, and he found it difficult to speak, he gulped some more water from his glass, and pulled out the keys to his farmhouse, and gave it to Meera, "It's all yours."

Some old memories had come back to haunt him; Mihir was feeling heavy hearted, he had to share, and he opened up, "Three years back, we were preparing for our return from our farmhouse to our home in the city. We were loading the luggage in our car, and my daughter, who was just two years old then, was playing near the gate, and unknowingly she went out of the gate. Suddenly a truck appeared from the blind turn and sped down towards her. Seeing that my wife fainted, I gathered her in my arms, and watched in horror, helplessly. My daughter was about to be rammed.

But God had different plans, suddenly our security guard's pet dog jumped upon my daughter and pushed her out of the way, and in the process, he got severely injured by the speeding truck.

I left my wife on a chair nearby and ran towards my daughter. The watchman too ran towards the road. My daughter had suffered a deep cut on her face, but otherwise she was fine, but the dog was motionless and covered in blood. I gave one of my cars' key to my watchman to take the dog to a veterinary doctor, while I rushed with my wife and daughter to the hospital in another car.

The dog was declared brought dead, and my wife too. Actually, the moment she saw the truck speeding towards our daughter, she died the same moment from massive heart failure. I couldn't save my wife, and would have lost my daughter too if that dog…

We didn't bury the dog; we got him cremated in *Kashi* with a pyre of sandalwood just beside the pyre of my wife. Their ashes were flown to be immersed in the river Ganga at *Haridwar*. We do his *shraad* every year, along with my wife's. The watchman refused to come back to that farmhouse, it was painful for him to be there without his four-legged friend around. I got him a piece of land in his village.

Even for me being in the city without her was tormenting, I shifted to the US with my daughter Akanksha. Akanksha still has that mark on her face, which she considers as her birthmark. Of course it was her second birth, and she considers the dog Moti, as her godfather. You know in our Hindu philosophy we should donate 10% of our earnings to others, yet, I live on 10% of my earning, and the remaining 90% goes to the NGO, of which I am the chairman."

Mihir, rubbed the ends of his eyes, near the nose, cleared his throat, and apologized for turning the atmosphere into a sad one. He got up to leave, and said, "The farmhouse has not been used since that day, though the watchman is the caretaker, and gets it cleaned every day. The pool has been dry since then, but I will make the necessary arrangement by tomorrow. You can use it the way you want to, and for the period you wish to.

You people are great, and if I can contribute anything in getting this Saint back to his healthy self, I will be more than happy to do it." He looked up at the sky as he uttered the last few words.

Papa walked up to Mihir, and gave him a bear hug, he needed it though he didn't realize it. That embrace broke his composure, and he started crying like a baby. Kabeer requested Meera to make some coffee for Mihir, while Mihir continued to cry on Papa's shoulder for almost five minutes. Then he collected himself and sat down on the sofa. Kabeer handed over a glass of water to Mihir.

Faith and Saint sat next to Mihir and stared at him with their tongues hanging out. As Mihir looked at them and smiled, Saint kept his foreleg on Mihir's lap and rubbed Mihir's stomach with his head. Mihir felt the warmth, and in turn rubbed Saint's head. The moment he did that, Saint jerked back his head.

Seeing all this, the mischievous Faith got into action. He jumped on to the sofa, planted himself next to Mihir and started licking his face and nose. Things got a bit better by the time coffee was served. Mihir helped himself with some cookies that were served along with the coffee. He thanked them for it, for everything this family and the gang have been doing.

After a while, he left; Papa had gone to see him off.

He came back with a message from Mihir for Kabeer. The message was that Mihir would be at his farmhouse early in the morning, and would get the arrangements done immediately. Kabeer should reach there before 11:00 because at 2:00 clock Mihir had to catch a flight for Mumbai. From Mumbai, he was scheduled to fly back to his home, USA. The message was immediately conveyed to Shivani and Pratima; both were super excited.

Next day, Kabeer went to the farmhouse along with Meera. Pratima and Shivani both had their prior commitments of feeding the dogs, so were unable to accompany him then. Meera had taken the first half of the day off from the office to accompany Kabeer.

It was a well-maintained farmhouse, with a lovely garden and lot of open space. Thick, dense trees surrounded the 15 feet high boundary walls. Mihir welcomed them into the hall, where they shared a cup of coffee. Post coffee Mihir took them to the backside of the farmhouse where the swimming pool was situated. The pool was filled with shimmering transparent water.

The shape of the swimming pool was oval, roughly thirty feet long and twelve feet wide. It was constructed thoughtfully for a family to enjoy and have fun. Of its thirty feet length, the first few feet were covered in a broad arc-shaped long stairs of roughly one-and-a-half feet each, and there were three such steps leading to the part where pool was just four feet deep. Depth of the pool ranged from four feet to fifteen feet across ends. On the sides there were metal stairs to climb out of the pool.

At regular intervals, there were hooks on the pavement, at the depth of six feet and ten feet. These hooks could be connected by a long rope with loops on the ends, to mark the spot from where the depth of the pool increased significantly. There was no provision for diving as it could be dangerous in the absence of a lifeguard, and handling mischievous kids was never easy. The pool area had a small changing room, and an open shower facility, which was fully functional. This ensured that the guests did not have to enter the main house with dripping bodies.

Mihir introduced the couple to Ramesh, the watchman cum caretaker, and in an apologetical manner took their leave; it was almost his time for departure. He had not shown the rest of the house to them, but had given the keys, and instructed Ramesh to help them whenever they needed his help. Ramesh was more than a watchman in this house; he was a caretaker who had his own separate quarters near the main gate. He also had the support of another watchman referred by him just to manage the gates at night. Ramesh was single, and though not a dog lover, he was comfortable with dogs.

Kabeer thanked Mihir earnestly, just as a hungry man would thank a kind person after being offered delicacies. Mihir was equally humble and kept insisting that if they required anything at all, they could call him on his USA number without any hesitation. Kabeer and Meera sat with Ramesh at the gate for some time as a token of courtesy and then started to take a walk around the farmhouse.

They discussed how God helped when one was in dire need. Just a day before yesterday they were told that a swimming pool was required, and today they had the keys to this entire farmhouse, and that too for an unlimited time. Meera too had to leave as she was scheduled for a meeting. Kabeer decided to tour the neighborhood while he waited for Dr Divya.

The place was not far away from Kabeer's residence, but it was quite off the main Ahmedabad city. It was still a village with its own STD code for the landline telephones. He saw that the people in the village were dressed in the traditional attire of dhoti, kurta and pagdi. The women on streets still kept their faces covered by the *ghunghat*. The concrete *pakka* road was only till the farmhouse, and beyond it was the *kachcha* dusty road.

The clock ticked 2:00 pm, and Dr Divya announced her arrival on the farmhouse. She was given a tour of the farmhouse like Mihir had given to Kabeer and Meera. She was quite happy and impressed about the arrangements, and certified it fit for Saint's swimming. Dr Divya and Kabeer left together for his home to have a look at the status of Saint's wounds and burns. Good news, she found that recovery was faster than expected, and they could start with the swimming lessons after two days' of precautionary gap.

The day for the first dip in the pool had arrived. After the morning walk for pee and poop, Saint and Faith were on their way to the farmhouse after having skipped the fetch-the-ball game. Kabeer was in Pratima's Range Rover with Saint; Meera and Shivani were in Meera's WagonR with Faith. It took hardly 15 minutes in the wee hours of no traffic to reach the farmhouse.

It was early, but Ramesh was already there waiting for them at the main gate. He was already in his uniform to attend to the special guests. Pratima and Meera parked the car inside the farmhouse and got down along with their dogs. Ramesh was astounded to see Saint, now that the wounds had recovered, and some hair had also grown back, he looked much better than what he looked when Mihir had met Saint. Some toys for the dogs were also brought along to stimulate Saint, in case if he showed lack of interest in getting into the pool, though they all wished that he really turned out to be an experienced swimmer.

Kabeer took off his shirt; his gym built body and the tattoo of a dog's paws on his chest was on display. There were three such paws decreasing in size, from right side of his chest to the left, with the punch line "walk in my heart". Kabeer entered the pool in his knee-length lose swimming costume with a beach print on it. He had tied his hair back in a pony and enjoyed the soothing cold waters. He had taken the stairs to step into the pool. And then moved backwards deeper in the pool.

He called out to the dogs to get into the pool, and Faith was so excited that he ran and jumped into the pool without being cautious. It was the first time for Faith to be in a swimming pool, yet within seconds he began to swim like a regular swimmer; he surely loved the pool.

However, Saint hesitated; his body language spoke of his dilemma. He was tempted by Kabeer and Faith's presence in the water, but at the same time, he was not sure about stepping in the pool. Kabeer moved up to the stairs and sat on the first step of the pool. Kabeer cajoled him to have trust and get in. Saint tried, he took first two steps, but instead of placing it on stairs he placed both his forelegs on Kabeer's lap. Kabeer very slowly slipped from first step to the next step, and took Saint along. Saint's all four legs, and his hips were immersed in the pool. He sat on the first step with his forelegs on Kabeer's lap. Again, at a slow pace, Kabeer moved from second step to the third and then the last one. By the time Saint reached the last step, he was already half immersed in the water. He had moved slowly and comfortably with Kabeer, but as soon as the water touched his torso, he froze for a few seconds and then ran back out of the pool into the lawn surrounding the pool. Without a doubt, he had never been to a swimming pool ever.

Meera tried to encourage Saint to head back to the pool, but he just sat there in the lawn clearly indicating that he was 'not interested'. Kabeer asked Meera for the ball they used in the morning for the fetch-the-ball game. Kabeer started playing the same game in the pool with Faith. He took the ball and threw it in the pool a little away from Faith. Faith swam towards the ball and fetched it back to Kabeer. Saint was watching it and was tempted to play his favorite morning game.

It was a deliberate attempt by Kabeer, he now threw the ball on the lawn at a distance from Saint. Saint immediately got into action and picked the ball. He ran back towards Kabeer but stopped at the brim of the pool. After a brief pause he threw the ball inside the pool, instead of entering the pool, towards Kabeer. All this was being captured by Pratima and Shivani in their respective phone cameras.

Now it was Faith's turn, Kabeer again threw the ball towards the deep end of the pool, which was fetched by Faith. Moving towards Saint, Kabeer threw the ball on the dry surface, but closer to the pool's pavement. Saint ran to fetch the ball, and returned. This time Saint reached the first step of the pool, and from there threw the ball back to Kabeer. Kabeer was happy with the progress, and now he planned to make the game more interesting; with rewards.

While Kabeer threw the ball to the other end of pool, Meera handed him the dog training treats. As soon as Faith got the ball back to him, Kabeer displayed the treat to Saint, and then gave it to Faith. Faith was ecstatic, while Saint stared at them; things were falling in place. Kabeer now threw the ball again to the dry area, close to the pool, and moved a little back towards the center of the pool.

Saint again ran to fetch the ball, and came down two steps into the pool but Kabeer was still far off to throw the ball back to him. Saint was in dilemma and Kabeer displayed the treats he had. Saint thought for some time, and then stepped further inside the pool until his entire body got drenched in the water. Everybody watched him in anticipation, wondering, what his next move would be, but then suddenly Saint started to retreat. Kabeer leapt towards him, and gave him few treats with lot of appreciation, this move stopped Saint from retreating.

Once Saint was apprcciatcd for his effort, immediately Kabeer provided him the support to take him deeper. Kabeer offered his lap for Saint's support. Faith too swam towards Saint, and started pulling him by his ear. This was exactly the same method that Faith had used while giving a tour of the house to Saint.

After initial hesitation Saint began to enjoy the water, and proactively made efforts to move in water; he started to swim. He was slow at first, and twice it looked like he was drowning.

But the more he swam the more confident he got. Saint's body harness with a long leash was still held loosely by Meera, while Kabeer and Faith swam on either sides of Saint. Saint finally reached the deep end of the pool, and turned around to swim back. This time Saint swam much better, and he reached the stairs at the other end of the pool in lesser time. He was joyous when he comfortably walked out of the pool. All the three girls came to him to appreciate with loud cheers. Saint jerked his body vigorously to get rid of the water, and that was enough to make all the girls' dresses wet. Thankfully, they were still in their morning attire of track-suits, and were to head back home from there.

Saint felt so delighted that he again went back to the pool, cautiously walked down the stairs, and swam to the center of the pool. Meera had removed the leash from the body harness, but the harness was still on Saint's body. Kabeer was still cautious, and he swam along with Saint. Meanwhile, Faith was in complete fun mood. He came to the left side of Saint, pulled his left ear towards him, and Saint followed Faith.

Saint spent fifteen minutes in the pool swimming, and then came out and sat on the dry lawn along with Faith. After a rest of around five minutes, Saint and Faith once again went back to the pool. While Faith had taken a leap from the side of the pool, Saint had chosen the arc-shaped stairs.

This time Kabeer kept himself in a corner at the deep end of the pool, and he threw the ball towards the other end of the pool. Saint and Faith swam, competing with each other, as they usually did to fetch the ball; but this time they were not running but swimming. Meera took a short video, and mailed it to Dr Divya, Dr Divya did not use Watsapp or any other chat application. After about half an hour, Saint followed by Faith came out of the pool. Both the dogs jerked off the water from their bodies and lay down on the lawn.

Kabeer came out and took his bag to the changing room. Meera prepared the morning meal for both the dogs, which they ate with great gusto, and again laid down. The sun was up, but it was fresh and soothing. There was still time for the sun to get into a hot summer mood. Kabeer had changed into jeans and a t-shirt. As he came out of the changing room, he turned towards the sun, took some water from the pool, and offered it to Lord Surya. With eyes shut and hands clasped, he offered his prayer.

Pratima had brought tea and some sandwiches from home, which was cherished by everyone as they sat beside Faith and Saint on the lawn. Sandwiches were also shared with Ramesh – the watchman cum caretaker. Saint and Faith had short hair (Saint was now in short hair because of the haircut) which dried quickly, but yet Kabeer rubbed their bodies with dry towels that he had brought for them. He then took them back to the car and thanked Ramesh again. Faith and Saint felt fresher than before, and during the entire journey back home they sat at the back of the car. They had a constant smile while they stared at the passing roads with their heads sneaking out of the car window. Kabeer decided that one day he will have his own personal swimming pool. Kabeer had swum after many years, and he now shared the same feeling of freshness with his four legged buddies.

Dr Divya saw the video and replied with a smiley that it looked good. She also mentioned that Saint would need much more than fifteen/thirty minutes sessions. "Hours" is the word she wrote in bold and underlined it too. After a couple of days, Saint began to spend more than an hour swimming in the pool and learnt to fetch the ball and float effortlessly in the pool. After a week, one fine day, Dr Divya joined the couple at the farmhouse to observe his performance live.

Pratima and Shivani had come for a couple of days and were back to their schedule, but now they had joined everyone on the 'inspection day' as Pratima had phrased it. Dr Divya was delighted with the performance, and as a reward treated both Faith and Saint with the special meal, she had made for the duo. Now she sat with all of them and confirmed that it was time to take it to the next level.

Saint's leg muscles were being exercised well, but now the exercise had to be more vigorous with more strength. So far, it has been like doing sit-ups where even when done a hundred times, it does not have the desired effect that twenty sit-ups with weights would achieve. Kabeer understood her point immediately, but he didn't know how to do that and so posed his question to Dr Divya.

Dr Divya replied, "First of all, Saint will require a bigger swimming area so that he is not required to turn around after short intervals. Managing turns with weight will slow down the entire workout." None of them understood what she was talking about. Then the doctor explained the entire procedure in a precise manner, and everyone agreed with their nods. But the problem they were again exposed to was how to find a bigger swimming pool.

What the doctor wanted was, almost double the size of the current pool that they were using. Dr Divya suggested that either a lake or a seashore would be the best bet for such exercises, but since there was nothing of that sort in Ahmedabad, Sabarmati River could be used. She knew an area which was much cleaner, and if the swimming was done in the middle of the river, then there would be absolutely no threat of infection. The area was Sabarmati Ashram, and she knew some people who could arrange permission.

Meera found it risky, but Kabeer placed his hand on Meera's knee in an assuring manner. Kabeer was a good swimmer, and he decided to take a few sessions in the river himself, before taking Saint in it. All agreed.

Kabeer dropped Meera and both the dogs home and went off for his own swimming classes. There he spoke to his coach regarding his problem and shook hands with him in agreement to what was discussed. The swimming pool was within the closed arena, and therefore, could be used even in the afternoon of summers. Kabeer had three days to achieve it. That was the deadline he had given himself. He went to the pool in the afternoon, and swam for more than two hours; he built his stamina and strength. Even in the gym he spent more time on endurance and strength building of his legs. He continued this for three days, and on the fourth day he went to the pool with some gym weights.

He wore a body harness that looked like a pistol holster to secure the gun beneath the armpits. He had an 'S' shaped metallic hook that was attached to his harness. Once in the water his coach attached a 10 kg lifting plate to this hook and dropped it in the waters. Kabeer flexed his legs and swam quite comfortably for 15 feet with the weight. He took a rest of 5 minutes, and again repeated the same exercise with 20kg weight. He could make it 12 feet this time. He now rested for almost 10 minutes, and then again entered with 40kg weight, and this time again made it to the 12 feet mark. His breath was heavy, but not exhausted.

He rested for 15 minutes, and once again tried with the 60 kg weight. But this time he could cover only 10 feet. He didn't like it, but his coach was impressed with the progress. Kabeer knew that this was not enough; the distance from the middle of the river to the shore was much more than 10 feet, and Saint weighed almost 200 pounds.

When Kabeer grunted in dismay, coach clarified that a three-day deadline was far too short for this goal to be achieved. His years of swimming practice were just stamina building efforts, but with the weights, he would need more time. He was upset with the doc, he wished that she had told him earlier, and he could have started his training much more before.

But, what was gone was gone. Saint and Faith were still being taken to the pool at the farmhouse, and for the time being Kabeer had started to tie ankle bands with weights attached to Saint's hind legs. He did this to assert more stress on his hind leg muscles (the ones used by a cyclist while practicing). But underwater, the weights lose their capacity quite significantly. It took 15 days for Kabeer to swim the 40 feet length of the pool with 100 kgs attached to his back. For the past couple of days, Meera had skipped office for an hour each day to observe

Kabeer practicing it. Severe practice made him get into a toned physique, and his stamina endured to the next level.

For Meera, this practice routine ended up with a byproduct which she loved; Kabeer had not smoked even a single cigarette for those fifteen days to secure his stamina, and strengthen his lungs.

It was a month now from the day Saint was rescued, his hair had started to grow back, and his tail looked bushy and thick. Saint and Faith spent their mornings comfortably by swimming for hours, it was a lot of fun. Faith had by himself developed underwater skills also, though he could do it only for some seconds. It had happened once when his treat fell into the pool and sank till the bottom of the pool at the deepest end. And Faith like a crazy bugger ducked his head in and tried to reach for the treat.

Kabeer had panicked when he saw Faith doing the gimmick. He too went underwater to get Faith out but to his amazement Faith with his own efforts had pushed his body down without any haste, reached for his treat, and then whooshed up to the surface. Post that moment, every day, Faith was given at least 10 such dips. Soon they began to blind fold his eye, and to throw the treat into the water and made Faith search for it. Apart from the fun, it was a perfect exercise for his brain and sniffing skills as well.

Saint had never tried this, and he would look at Faith with bored eyes whenever Faith played underwater. There seemed to be a visible improvement in Saint's limping, and even at home, he managed to play for longer durations. It was probably the last day for them to use the farmhouse pool; the arrangements had been made for the river experiment for the next day.

Kabeer had arranged two big boats for the day and had assured the boatmen that if things went well, then the boats could be hired for a longer period and on a monthly basis. The time to reach the Sabarmati Ashram was 6:30 am, and Dr Divya was to be picked from her home on the way. Kabeer himself had crossed the river twice with the 100kg weight hooked to him before the 'D' Day. As per their routine they had woken-up at 5:30 am, but instead of taking Faith and Saint for their morning walks and then to the farmhouse, today they drove towards Sabarmati Ashram.

This time Mummy and Papa had also joined. Meera, Mummy and Papa were in WagonR, and Dr Divya was to be picked by Meera. Pratima had come with Shivani and picked Kabeer, Saint and Faith in her Range Rover. She freed some space in the back by adjusting the backrest of the backseat. Kabeer was rather silent throughout the journey. Only Pratima knew the reason why. Had Meera been in the same car, she would have been sure what Kabeer was doing – chanting the Mahamritunjay mantra.

Kabeer had a deep and strong belief in the power of this mantra, and he used it very rarely, and only during important moments of his life. Most importantly, he always chanted for someone else and never for himself.

It was 6:30 am, and everybody had arrived. The boatmen had reached by 6 'O' clock itself. Faith was readied with his regular body harness and a strong leash, but for Saint, the preparation was different from his first preparation for the swimming session. It was a spontaneous decision of Dr Divya to first try the activity with Faith. That was because Faith was a natural swimmer, and had swum from the first time itself like a pro. Secondly, Faith was light in weight; and if required he could be pulled out easily. Finally, after observing Faith, Saint would drop his inhibitions and would enter the river with a very positive frame of mind.

Everybody agreed. Kabeer took off his t-shirt. Every muscle of his upper body could be counted. The silver pendant in shape of a trishul with a damru, displayed on his chest was shining brighter than the sun. He had worn a short mid-thigh swimming costume. His thighs had developed some muscles which Kabeer himself had never known earlier. Kabeer had tied his hair in a bun over the head, and rest of the hair cascaded down his shoulder. Before boarding the boat Kabeer had washed his hands and feet with the water. He then bowed his head to the river by touching the shore where the river met the ground. Faith and Kabeer took one of the two boats to a short distance from the shore, where the water was absolutely clean. Though the shore was also quite clean, there were some rotten things which had floated to the shores.

First, Kabeer went into the water, and then Faith walked on Kabeer's body. Faith was unexpectedly calm about the new adventure. Kabeer gradually brought Faith's legs into the water. Kabeer's heart beat hard as if he had been running a marathon. He wanted to stay calm as he did not want to transfer his nervousness to Faith. He looked up at the sky, closed his eyes and sought his help with a loud roar of – 'MAHADEEEEEEEEEEEEV' (MAHADEV). Everybody on the shore repeated after him as loudly as they could with their hands raised in the air. Saint too let out a howl, with his neck craned, and head pointing to the sky. He had his eyes closed.

Kabeer allowed Faith's body to slide into the river but held on to the leash tightly gripped in his fist. He allowed a length of about two feet free so that Faith could explore. Faith with his entire body immersed in the river, except for his head and got his legs in action. He stayed afloat, and then gradually started to move forward as much as the leash allowed him to do so. Kabeer freed the leash some more and held on only to the end of the leash loop.

Faith swam a bit further, and then Kabeer got his arm hooked inside the loop till his shoulder, and started to swim along with Faith. They both had swum for a little more than 50 feet when Kabeer asked Faith to turn around. Faith turned and tried to get back to the boat. By now they both had begun to swim against the slow current of the river. Everyone clapped and cheered for them, and Saint started to bark and jump with excitement on the shore.

Dr Divya's logic had worked, Saint was now eager to get into the river. Kabeer and Faith had by now reached the boat. Upon Kabeer's instructions, Faith got on to his shoulder and then climbed into the boat with a leap. Kabeer climbed into the boat from the side, while the boatman had remained on the other side to keep the balance of the boat. The boat was rowed back to the shore, where Meera was ready with special treats for Faith. Saint was in haste to get to the boat, and was not happy when Kabeer stopped him. He had to be readied for the exercise, and this time in a different manner.

Kabeer too had to ready himself with his body harness on which he had hooked the weights. But, this time a ten-foot-long and strong leash was hooked to the harness, and the other end of the leash was hooked to a special harness worn by Saint.

Saint's harness covered his torso completely and was wrapped and zipped on his back. The harness held Saint from the chest. Around his body were like two jackets worn, one on top and another at the bottom. Both these jackets had loops at the joints where legs met the torso, this was to ensure that in case of emergency, these extra leashes could be hooked on to, and then Saint could be pulled out by the boatmen. Kabeer once again prayed to the river God with folded hands, and then got into the boat with Saint.

Kabeer felt restless and needed his Lord to be with him. He started to sing the *Shiv Tandav Stotram* in his heart, without a sound but only his lips moving silently. "*Jatatavigalajjala prabhava paavitasthale, galevlamb lambitang bhujangtunmalikam, damadamad damadamd ninadvaddamarvayam, chakar chand tandavam tano tu nah shivah shivam...*" But it was so loud in his heart that it could be heard by Meera and Papa, they both also started chanting 'Shiva, Shiva' in their hearts.

The boat reached the same spot as earlier, and Kabeer looked up at the sky, and picked his silver pendant and kissed it. Then he got into the river. The boatman reached the other corner of the boat, opposite to the side from where Saint was to get down into the river. Saint placed his forelegs on Kabeer's chest and his hind legs on the edge of the boat and jumped. This movement pushed the boat and Kabeer in opposite directions, and Saint landed his hind legs into the river.

Kabeer gradually let go off Saint's forelegs also. Slowly Saint began to float, and there was a broad smile on his face. He floated effortlessly. Saint instead of moving in any direction, kept making rounds at the same spot, looking in all directions, and soon reached near Kabeer. He looked at his gang standing on the shore and barked twice (as if saying 'love you'), looked at the boatman and barked once (thanks), and then looked at Kabeer and licked (kiss) his face.

Kabeer observed Saint's happiness. Saint gazed up at the sky, at the sun, and then closed his eyes and dropped his head inside the river. His entire body was inside the river now, and the leash tightened on Kabeer's harness, but Kabeer did not panic; Saint's tail swayed just like a warrior's victory flag above the surface of the water. Gradually his tail started to move forward. Yes, Saint was doing an under-water swim and that too against the river current. After a few seconds, Saint brought his head out and began to swim. Kabeer kept himself afloat, and Saint dragged him along because of the attached leash.

It was after fifteen minutes of utmost patience on Faith's part when he realized that everybody had forgotten him, and so he started to bark loudly. He felt that those hours in the pool were better than the few minutes in the river. Kabeer signaled the boatman to bring Faith also, which the boatman did.

As the boat stopped in the middle of the river, Faith jumped into the river and began swimming towards Saint. Faith bit Saint a little harder than usual on his nose and barked. Saint licked Faith's ear, and then both of them began to swim, followed by Kabeer. After an hour of swimming, all of them headed back to the boat. Kabeer was not tired by the long duration of this exercise as he had not worked any of his muscle. He was dragged by Saint for some time, and then he had switched the other end of the leash from Saint to Faith. Though it took efforts from Faith, even he could take Kabeer around in the river. For both the dogs the soft flow of the river did not matter.

The boatmen rowed all three of them back to the shore, where everyone was seated with tea which Meera had carried in a thermos and sandwiches were made by Pratima. Dr Divya held in her hand homemade meals for both the super dogs. Everybody welcomed the trio with claps. Everyone's heart was warm, their eyes were moist, and throats dry. Kabeer stepped out of the boat last. He had finalized the hiring of the boat for the entire month. Kabeer probably had tears in his eyes, but no one could be sure because the water was still flowing down from his knotted hair bun.

Meera walked to him and hugged him tightly. Kabeer hugged her back with an equal embrace. Meera could understand from the tight hug, that Kabeer was in an emotionally charged state of mind, she whispered in his ears, "I am so proud of you, my man. I know I was wrong when I did not agree with your decision to quit your job, but what you are doing now makes me so happy to be wrong. You are my hero, now I am sure that all my Monday fasts have reaped the fruits by having you here, beside me. I Love You Kabri." (Kabri was the nickname for him used only by Meera, especially when she felt romantically high) It was for the first time that they both had hugged each other outside the privacy of their room, but the moment was highly emotional and demanded it.

They both walked back together, but were looking so opposite in their looks. Meera in her tracksuit and Kabeer in his swimming costume, Meera a cute and lovely face of milky complexion with her hair in a pony wearing small earing in her ears, and Kabeer with a bun on his head and lose hair behind his back, beard almost five inches on his face a ripped husky colored body with strangest tattoos on. Meera looked couple of years younger to her age and Kabeer at least 5 years older. Meera a 5 feet 2 inches 60 kgs doll and Kabeer 5 feet 10 inches 80 kgs demon. As soon as they both reached the gang, Pratima poured his coffee brought by Meera in a separate kettle, Papa got up from his seat pulled out a Rs 500/- note from his pocket circled the hand holding the note over the couple's head and handed it to mummy; it would be given to someone needy on the way back.

Once the drinks were complete and the dog duo had fallen asleep under the shade of the tree, Dr Divya charged in, “It's great that things are falling in place, thanks to Kabeer and praise to the Lord. But what happened today was just a test to check if required exercise can be done or not. Fortunately, the answer is yes. Kabeer I don't know how long it will take, but the exercises I have specified needs to be done on a daily basis for at least two hours, and after few weeks take it to three hours. Faith will not be OK if you and Saint are out for the whole morning without him.

Also, you have your work to attend to. So, how do you plan to do this every day?” Kabeer was on a panel as a consultant with a renowned strategic consultancy firm – CPMG. He had taken a month off after resigning from his job, and the month was over.

Before Kabeer could answer, Meera broke-in, “The work can wait for one more month. He is no more an employee, as he did not want to be one in the first place. I will get ready early every morning, while Papa and Kabeer can take the dogs out for the morning walks. We will then adjust the space in the WagonR so that it will be sufficient for both Saint and Faith to be brought here. I too will come with Kabeer daily here, and while going back, Kabeer will drop me at my office. On the days I can't accompany him, Papa will come. Right, Papa?”

Papa replied, “Beta, I would suggest that I will come daily. I reach the court by 11:00 only and have ample time to go back and get ready for my work. Your office starts early, so only on those days when I can't accompany him, you accompany Kabeer.”

Kabeer smiled at Dr Divya, “Mam, do you still think that there is a problem?”

Dr Divya replied with amazement, “The entire family is mad for these four-legged lives, and many people think, ‘what they do is something nobody else can do’. Anyways, I am glad that you made me a part of your gang. And on the days when it's possible, I would accompany you. Anyway I need to supervise the activities of the three musketeers here in the open nature." To which everybody laughed wholeheartedly. They found the tag of 'three musketeers', given by Dr Divya quite amusing. The laughter woke-up the peacefully sleeping gangsters and they started to make a ruckus for the long drive to home.

Next day Kabeer and Meera reached the place with Faith and Saint only to find that the boatman had a different kind of a boat this time. The boat did not have a railing at the one end, and it looked like a sort of a ramp for cars. When Kabeer asked the boatman about it, the boatman explained that after witnessing previous day's activity, he thought that this boat would be perfectly suitable. Both the dogs can step into the river from the rare end of the boat. Then he showed a ladder made of thick ropes. He added that the rope would help them to grip their paws while getting in and out of the boat. This way a lot of trouble could be saved. Meera's smiled broadened, and she commented, "Smart Man... hah....", and Kabeer hugged the boatman for being so thoughtful about the dogs.

Saint and Faith both had their single body harness on, and long leashes were attached to both their harnesses. The other end of these leashes was hooked on to Kabeer's own body harness. While they walked down towards the shore, they looked comical. All three of them have worn the body harness, they all looked alike. Meera clicked this rare sight and posted it on Facebook. She tagged the gang members with the title – The Three Musketeers 😆!!!

As the boatman had rightly said, the task of getting into the water turned out to be as smooth as for the deep-sea divers. After they had swum for around 15 minutes, Kabeer removed Saint's leash from his own harness and hooked it to the loop attached to the helm of the boat. Now Kabeer and Faith started to swim a little fast and indicated to Saint to follow suit. Saint had to swim hard to reach them as he was to pull the boat behind him.

As soon as the leash tightened, Kabeer would start his instruction – "PULL. PULL my boy PULL." Saint was not trained for this sort of command, but when he started to pull and heard the word 'PULL' in an appreciative fashion. He began to understand that when the word 'PULL' was commanded, he needs to pull things, and that would make his master happy. This is the way normally all the commands to dogs are taught. Even basic commands like 'sit' and 'stop' and 'run' are learnt by dogs in the same manner.

It took around 10 days for Saint to reach a stage where he didn't have to work that hard to pull the boat and was able to match the swimming speed of Faith and Kabeer. Swimming puts your limbs on a workout, especially the legs. For dogs, the muscles of their hind legs are required to be flexed. So, while swimming and pulling the weight, Saint had to work his hind legs hard to move in the water, and in turn, this strengthened his hind leg muscles.

The protein content in the diet for Saint was significantly increased and included more pulses for the evening feed with extra egg whites in the morning after the swimming exercise. Saint's muscles started to develop and tighten, including the hip muscles. As a result, the hip joint was secured naturally in its righteous position and held tightly with firm muscles.

Once Saint began to comfortably pull the boat, Meera started boarding the boat to increase the weight of the boat. Later, they started the task of swimming more and more against the river currents. The plan was clear that as soon as Saint's strength and endurance increased, the weight of the boat had to be increased, and this they did by placing big stones and rocks. It was ensured that Saint had to swim really hard to manage a normal speed, though once in a while he was allowed a free swim as well.

After a month of water exercise, not only had the limping significantly reduced, but even the X-ray confirmed that the bones had moved well in place of the joint. The muscles seemed much stronger compared to what the X-ray had revealed two months back.

The reduced limping made Hip Dysplasia look like a temporary injury, and the muscles in the hind portion of Saint looked bigger and stronger. Faith being sparsely coated with hair, his muscle matched with that of an athletic wrestler. Saint's hair had grown longer, and he looked more handsome now.

On the riverfront, the old raft like the boat was replaced by a bigger boat, but the same routine of adding weights, whenever Saint got comfortable was continued. Raju, the boatman, had become a great friend of them by now and had also developed a secret crush on Pratima. When Kabeer shared this with the gang, everyone playfully pulled Pratima's leg. It was her sporting nature that made her take it lightly, and not get mad at them. She allowed them to tease her about the simple boatman. Pratima had also felt that there was something different when Raju looked at her, but she knew that it was nothing harmful, or meant to be demeaning. Thrice the gang had eaten together with Raju. Twice by the riverside, and once they had taken Raju to a restaurant for lunch.

It was now three months since the swimming exercise had started. The summer season had ended, and monsoon was nearing. This delayed the morning timings, and it became difficult for Meera to manage. So Papa had started to accompany Kabeer and the dogs regularly. In these three months, they had skipped the exercise for about seven days. Pratima, Shivani and Dr Divya had visited 10 to 12 times. The dedication and perseverance that Kabeer had shown was a pure expression of his passion and love for dogs. Kabeer was known for his passion in whatever he did, be it office, gym, swimming. Even the hours he used to spend late nights for his consultancy work with CPMG depicted his passion.

The X- ray reports confirmed that the joint was completely in place, and the limping had vanished entirely. Dr Divya suggested that now for another month swimming on alternative days would be OK. Then after a month, they should reduce it to just twice a week. She cautioned that twice a week had to be followed, and now the weights ought not to be increased too much. Instead of making Saint work really hard to pull, just make it 'not easy' to pull. By now Saint who had weighed a whopping 100 kgs had lost three kilos. He would have lost lot of fats as even after developing humongous muscles, he was just 3kgs lighter. His coat was back to its original form, this time shinier and denser. His eyes were brighter too, and he played more often, bothered more, ate more, and there was more of every good thing.

On his first off from the swimming schedule, Kabeer took Saint back to the place where he was found abandoned. Though there was a serious discussion at home that it might upset Saint and his fears and remembrance of those few troubled days may bring him down emotionally. Even Dr Divya had presumed that he might feel about to be abandoned again. However, Kabeer had full trust in his bonding with Saint. He also planned to take Faith along. As usual, everyone surrendered to Kabeer's wish.

When Saint reached the spot where he was left abandoned, he stared deep into Kabeer's eyes. Kabeer came out of the car and got Faith out of the car too. Saint followed them unleashed. This was the first time he walked without a leash on the road. Kabeer always left both of them free without a leash at home, but on the road–never. Anything could excite them for a chase, and the vehicles on the roads sometimes end up ending lives.

Saint stared into Faith's eyes, and then made a soft whining sound followed by a low bark. Kabeer removed Faith's leash too. Saint pulled Faith's ear and made him follow him; Kabeer followed them. He recalled that particular day; it was a tough but lucky day. And the night was a scary one, though beautiful at the same time.

Saint sat there, at the same spot, for some time and sniffed around. Faith followed his example and copied everything he did. Kabeer ensured that though he was lost in his own thoughts, he should not lag too far behind. He wanted to be within the comfortable reach of Saint, to assure that history wouldn't repeat itself. After they roamed around a bit, Kabeer put the leash around both the dogs and walked towards the village.

Kabeer asked a villager about the milkman with the motorcycle. Probably there was only one milkman in the entire village; Kabeer made it to his place without much trouble. The milkman was unfortunately not there at that point of time, as he had gone to the city for some work. The security guard refused to allow the dogs inside the cowshed. Kabeer tipped him generously with a one thousand rupee note, and then the worker allowed the three of them to enter the shed, but on one condition that the cattle should not be disturbed.

Kabeer went in first and started to move slowly around where cattle were tied. Faith and Saint too walked slowly, when Saint abruptly stopped – Faith… He too stopped, and Kabeer also stopped. Saint kept looking in one direction, and after almost five to seven minutes, a slightly grown up calf ran towards them. Faith felt intimidated, but because Saint was sitting silently with his tongue hanging loose, Faith controlled his nerves. The calf slowed down and stood still, face-to-face with Saint. The worker watched this amazing sight and took out his smart phone. Kabeer smiled wryly, and asked the worker, "Is it a ritual to shoot a video of this dog every time he is seen by you people?"

The poor worker could not understand his satire as he was not aware that the milkman too, had shot a video of Saint earlier. Thanks to his video that the plight of Saint had come under the spotlight. If not for that video no one would have known about Saint's abandonment. Saint licked the calf for some time, and then made some sound. The calf in reply made its typical calf sound. Faith looked at both of them turning his head in amazement, and then went on to lick the calf, but the calf ran back to its shed. Saint's eyes followed the calf till it reached its mother.

Within a few minutes, the cow tried to come towards Saint, but she was tied. Kabeer took both his buddies to the cow. Cow swung her horns, and Saint raised his paw to touch them. A continuous gaze of calf and mother cow on Saint, and Saint's on both of them brought a smile on Kabeer's face. Saint moved ahead and gave a final lick to the mother cow and the calf as a goodbye signal. Saint was also sporting the same constant smile on his face when he moved back followed by Faith and Kabeer.

By the time they reached back to the place where the car was parked, there was some movement and little traffic on the road. Local residents were heading to their place of work. Suddenly the same laborer passed by with his son – Pappu. It was Pappu who recognized Saint and called for him. The laborer and Kabeer greeted each other, both were happy for Saint and thanked each other and gave credit to each other. Kabeer asked if he would allow his son Pappu to play with Saint for a little while. Initially, the laborer was little hesitant, but later when he was assured by Kabeer, he permitted.

Kabeer took the kid in his arms and walked back to Saint. Saint sat down on his hind legs and began to smell the kid, Faith once again copied him. Saint's eyes were moist, or it could have been Kabeer's imagination. Saint seemed calm while playing; he rubbed the kid's tummy, and his feet with a cold nose and the kid broke into laughter. Saint was ecstatic, and his smile broadened. Faith copied Saint here also, though Faith felt nothing overwhelming. Nevertheless, he once again imitated Saint and smiled broadly.

Pappu's father asked if he too could go near the dogs. Kabeer laughingly invited him to do so. Now the son was in his father's arms, and father sat next to Saint. He was on one knee. Saint smelled the father, licked him once, and then turned his attention to the kid again. Again Faith copied him 😂. The father had tears in his eyes; he recalled the way Saint had behaved earlier, and now in around four months, Saint had changed so much. The father felt happy that he was able to play with Saint, which was something he couldn't imagine doing until that day.

He had one more wish pending of that day. He wanted to feed Saint from his tiffin. He put forward his wish to Kabeer, and Kabeer felt so moved by the man's warmth and simplicity. Kabeer asked him to fetch his tiffin box. The man went to bring it, and all the time the kid in his own arms. The father realized soon that Saint's love for his son was still intact, though not his possessiveness.

The father opened the lid of his tiffin box and offered a roti to Saint. Saint first glanced at Kabeer for permission. Kabeer just nodded smilingly, and Saint ate the roti and then started to look into the tiffin box for more Rotis. Tears rolled down the man's face, and he offered him yet another roti, but before the calm Saint could eat it, Faith snatched the roti and ate it. Kabeer laughed, and so did the man and his young son. And Faith?.... No, faith didn't copy. Faith copied only Saint, and that too because he was new to that area, and he could only understand that Saint had been here earlier. He did not know anything else; he did exactly what Saint did. After the meal, the labourer took leave of Kabeer and started his journey. Once he sat astride the cycle, he asked Kabeer in a loud voice, "What's his name?"

Kabeer replied, "Saint. The Saint."

The man replied as he paddled the cycle, "He looks like a stalwart. The Stalwart."

Kabeer smiled and repeated the two names in a whispering sound – The Saint. The Stalwart.

Saint gets his Habitat

Kabeer returned home, and everybody was glad to see Saint smiling and back home playing with his mate Faith. Kabeer got ready, took his breakfast of *aloo parathe* and *lassi*, and shortly after that left for CPMG office. He was scheduled for an important presentation. He was dressed in his Saturday attire of denim trousers with a shirt and a blazer. The two-hour presentation went off well in the conference room of the office. One of the NBFC (Non-Banking Financial Corporation – these are companies which provide loans, but cannot source deposits through bank accounts like any bank would do.) had got a banking license and had hired CPMG to plan a strategy for their sales force.

Kabeer, in spite of having huge experience, had worked hard for this project, and his hard work had paid off. The clients were happy, and CPMG was happier. Clients had attended his presentation and then moved on for lunch hosted by CPMG. Once the clients left, the top brass of CPMG decided to celebrate the success and took the entire team to Abu directly.

Once in Abu, everybody got drunk, including Kabeer, and out of nowhere, the topic of dogs popped up. One of the director's son-in-law was a veterinary doctor in Toronto – Canada. The director, Mr Sinha, also lived in Toronto and had specially flown down to India for the NBFC presentation. It was Mr Sinha's first interaction with Kabeer, and he was not aware of what Kabeer did, apart from his contractual services with CPMG. Kabeer became an active participant in the discussion about dogs. Then the discussion moved on to the different breeds of dogs. It started with the most popular breed in India, the Labrador, and then moved to the not so popular breeds like St. Bernard, Siberian husky and Akita.

Mr Sinha's talk about St. Bernards was so factual that it steered Kabeer's thoughts in a different direction. According to Mr Sinha, St. Bernard was a breed of dog belonging to the utmost cold climate, where the temperatures were usually subzero. And indeed that was the natural habitat of St. Bernard. Unfortunately, people in India think it is sufficient if their St. Bernard was kept in an ordinary air-conditioned room. Kabeer had nothing to counter that statement because it was a fact, and he had a St. Bernard in an air-conditioned room in his own home.

Kabeer had many times forgotten to keep his Saint 24 hours in the air-conditioned room. Many times Saint had to draw the attention of the family to switch on the air conditioner. This habit of his was found rather cute. The bottom line was that Saint was being kept in an unnatural habitat, and it was actually a criminal thing to do. Kabeer went silent, and his thoughts got disconnected from the discussion and meandered to his own Saint. The booze party and the dinner was done before all retired to their respective rooms.

Everybody slept like a log, but Kabeer could not sleep, even though he had consumed a decent amount of alcohol. Next day, post breakfast, they all started for their return journey to Ahmedabad. Throughout the journey, Kabeer was lost in his thoughts with his eyes shut. Everyone thought that he was fast asleep because of the excess drinking the previous night. But realty was that he had not been able to sleep even for a minute.

By 1:00 pm, he was back home, and everyone sensed his mood correctly. He loved both Faith and Saint equally, but that day he showered more love on Saint. Meera gauged that his bad mood had something to do with Saint. Meera decided to keep the discussion for later, and congratulated him for his first success as an entrepreneur. Kabeer had lunch with everyone at home as it was a Sunday, and soon everyone had gone for the afternoon nap; which was like a Sunday ritual.

Before Meera could begin the discussion, Kabeer himself brought up the topic and said how a discussion about the natural habitat of St. Bernards made him feel that it's unfair to keep Saint in such climatic conditions. Meera could not imagine life without Saint, and Faith would go mad without his friend. The discussion was long and deep, and less weightage was given to their emotions, and for Faith, it was decided that they would adopt another dog. In the end, they both agreed that Saint should be sent to a permanent home somewhere in the north of India like Ladakh.

Over evening tea, the same topic was discussed with both Mummy and Papa. Mummy and Papa's sorrow could be felt even by the dogs as they stopped playing and sat with the family. Later in the evening, Pratima and Shivani were also informed about their discussion, and the girls agreed with the difficult decision with heavy hearts. Dr Divya was not available as she, along with her husband, had gone for a religious pilgrim, and had left all means of communication behind. It was more of a meditative rehab rather than a pilgrim.

It didn't turn out to be difficult for Kabeer to find a home for Saint. Like everything after Saint's rescue kept falling in place, even finding his new home happened the same way. Kabeer had a Punjabi friend called Hridaydeep Arora, whose sister was married to a Lt. Commander in the Army, and as luck would have it, they were currently posted in Ladakh. Coincidentally they were keen to adopt a dog to give company to their twelve-year-old German Shepherd. The lieutenant had had a hard time finding a suitable dog for adoption, as he wanted a breed that could survive the brutal winter of Ladakh, and what better breed could that be, than a St. Bernard. Here too God made the arrangement within a day, just as HE had arranged for the swimming pool.

There was a special plane for only army personnel, which was departing from Mumbai to Ladakh, scheduled for departure on coming Friday, and the lieutenant had got all the necessary travel arrangements and documentation done for Saint's relocation.

A big carrier was arranged to take Saint from Ahmedabad to Mumbai by road. On Tuesday Kabeer and Meera went with Hridaydeep to inspect the carrier, which was actually a big cargo container that is generally used for supplies sent from railway stations and seaports. It was literally converted into a small house for Saint. It had a 4-ton air conditioner, a big bed, two large bowls fixed to the base of the container, and lot of toys. The entire container had been arranged in such a way that the walls up to the height of three feet were padded with a thick cushion material; even if by mistake Saint bangs against the walls, he won't get hurt.

Kabeer and Meera found that the arrangements were more than what they had expected. However, to make it easier for Saint, it was decided that for the next two days Kabeer and Saint would have a practice session travelling in the container for about four to five hours, and they would be able to gauge if Saint was comfortable in the container. This was to ensure that he would be able to endure the eight hour road journey from Ahmedabad to Mumbai.

Next day Kabeer took Saint, without Faith to the container, and climbed in; Saint got in with the help of a ramp. The air conditioner had been switched on an hour back, which had made it colder than the home air conditioners ever could. Saint stared at the air conditioner for a long time, and then started to run, dance and jump around in the container; it was a travelling saloon.

Kabeer felt better and more confident about his decision. They traveled for three hours in the container, he knew the route they were on, and it had its share of potholes too, but the jolts were not felt inside the container. In fact, it was as good as 1st Class AC compartment of a Rajdhani Express.

During these three hours, Saint played for around half an hour and then slept. He slept like never before on the bed that was provided. Kabeer sat opposite with his back against the wall of the container. Kabeer's eyes were so fixed on Saint; that he had forgotten to blink for quite some time. He was completely unaware of the tears that rolled from his bloodshot red eyes. After three hours the door of the container were opened, and Saint instead of running out just woke up and sat on his bed. It was only when Kabeer got out of the container to walk down the ramp that he got down from his bed, and walked down the ramp, and then ran with Kabeer to jump into the car.

Kabeer had taken some videos and pictures of Saint playing and sleeping on the bed, inside the container. The entire gang had mixed feelings of joy and sorrow about Saint leaving them to a place more suitable for his existence. The cooler container had made Saint so comfortable there; that they could easily imagine how wonderful he would feel in the snow covered open areas of Ladakh.

The next day Kabeer took Saint once again to travel in the container. Saint was like eager to get in. Once the ramp was placed, Saint just looked at Kabeer for his permission, and then with a slight nod from Kabeer, he ran into the container and jumped on his bed. There was nothing special about the bed, but the extra cold container helped him to enjoy the bed, whereas at home he found floor cooler than the bed, and therefore, always slept on the floor. Once Kabeer was inside, the door of the container was closed, and the trip started. Once again, Saint ran, and jumped, and danced for some time, then dropped himself on the bed for a lovely nap. Now Kabeer was fully confident of the things falling in place. Kabeer had worn his leather jacket, which made it comfortable for him to be in the cold container.

After the trip, Kabeer once again thanked Hridaydeep and expressed how grateful he felt to have a friend like him. But Kabeer seemed quite low, and his friend very well knew the reason. The evening was very silent at Kabeer's home, except for the two mischievous dogs. Papa had not even heard the news and had taken an extra couple of pegs of whiskey compared to his normal routine. Coming day, Saint was scheduled for an early morning departure, so everybody decided to go to bed early, but then, nobody could sleep that night.

Kabeer had dropped a message about Saint's time of departure to all the members of the gang, and everybody had gathered at Kabeer's residence in the wee hours to bid their final goodbye. Dr Divya was still missing as she was not yet back from her tour. As decided, Kabeer alone accompanied Saint to the place from where the journey was to start.

Everything was ready there, Kabeer arrived a little before the departure time, Hridaydeep was already there. Kabeer and Saint got inside the container, he thought of spending a few additional minutes with Saint before they parted. Hridaydeep stood outside and was talking to the defense personnel. Saint started his routine of jumping, dancing and running around the container. The moment he climbed on to the bed to sleep, Hridaydeep signaled Kabeer that it was time to leave.

Kabeer kissed the snoring Saint on his forehead and walked down the ramp with the heavy legs; he had never felt that way ever before. He felt the weight of the entire Mt. Everest had been tied to his boots, and he was dragging his feet out of the container down the ramp.

Once Kabeer was out, they removed the ramp and closed the door of the cabin. It was the first time that Kabeer saw the doors being closed, standing outside the truck. Doors were not as strong as the other walls but much stronger than the routine shutters. The truck moved with the container slowly towards its destination, Mumbai and Kabeer drove back to his home.

He didn't want to be alone, he wanted Saint, but Saint had to go. Kabeer felt the urge to go and hug Faith tightly, but it was still time for him to be with Faith. Kabeer lit his first cigarette after a gap of months, and then took deep drags back to back, hard. This was the first time he smoked since he had started his swimming practice with the weights. The cigarette finally had its effect with a temporary slowdown of his raging emotions.

He reached home, and Meera was at the door, she hugged him sideways, and could smell the cigarette. She was not happy about it, but she didn't say anything. Kabeer sat on the sofa and called out for Faith, who was still near the door of the room. Faith kept staring at the main door expecting Saint to walk in, but there was no Saint to walk-in. When Kabeer called him again, he got up and ran, but surpassed him to reach the main door, and started to bark but in a joyous tone. Meera turned back and saw, it was Dr Divya standing there.

She was for the first time seen in a salwar suit, instead of her routine jeans and *kurta*. She had a small bag in her hand. She walked in and embraced Faith and kept looking inside the house, waiting for Saint. When Saint didn't come, she called out his name, in vain. It was then that Kabeer got up from the sofa and told Dr Divya, "Saint has gone to his natural habitat."

Dr Divya, "What natural habitat? Your sense of humor has gone bad Kabeer." She again called for Saint in a loud voice.

Meera said, "Saint is going to Laddakh today, Kabeer just dropped him off."

Dr Divya turned to Kabeer, "What is this?" Then she looked around with a frown at everyone, and asked, "Will somebody tell me as what is happening? What is being done to my patient without my knowledge?"

Kabeer told everything in brief, and ended by saying, ".... And that's why he is not here."

Dr Divya was in a rage and slapped Kabeer as hard as she could do with her delicate hand. She shouted, "Who the hell you think you are? Einstein? Newton? I will tell you what you are; you are an IDIOT & A BRAINLESS ASS..."

She glared at everybody, and continued, "Do you even understand that Saint is technically again abandoned by YOU PEOPLE. Mr Kabeer Kapoor, the Saint, trusted you with lot of fear, and today you have made his fear come true again. After being abandoned by his master Saint thought that you would never ever leave him, and now you have again left him, YOU

CRAZY FELLOW...Where did you drop him? Which route are these guys taking? We need to stop them right now. Kabeer move immediately before I do something to you."

Kabeer and Dr Divya ran out, Meera too sprinted and joined them. Mummy turned and went to the small temple in the house, and started to pray hard. Papa called up Pratima and Shivani to update them. Kabeer knew that they must have reached the Ahmedabad – Baroda Expressway by now, and probably would have reached the toll booth by now. The traffic was scarce, and so Dr Divya drove her Scorpio like a pro car racer. On a couple of turns, she had almost tumbled her car. Pratima and Shivani also drove towards the expressway in Pratima's Range Rover. Throughout the journey, Kabeer kept smoking one stick after another, and Dr Divya lectured him peppered with curses and colourful abuses.

Dr Divya screamed at the top of her voice, "Kabeer, Natural Habitat Is Only A Physical Requirement. What About The Emotional Requirement? You Know Better Then Me, What Saint Has Gone Through. He Had Never Been With Somebody Un-Known Without You Being With Him. How Could You Even Think That He Will Be Able To Survive Without You? You Will Adopt Another Dog, But Will Saint Ever Be Able To Accept Another Master? A Stranger, In A Strange Place? Do You Think That Saint Bernards Require Only Cold Weather To Survive? And They Have No Emotional Needs? He Is Almost Six Yrs And Has Wonderfully Lived Without Cold Weather." Dr Divya was completely right.

Kabeer tried to reason, "But Divya you should have seen the way he played and slept in that cold container. He was so happy to be in such a cold place."

Dr Divya again screamed back at him, "That's Because You Were There With Him. Even When He Slept, He Knew You Were There With Him. When He Woke Up He Saw You And Did Not Panic. He For Sure Would Have Woken Up By Now,

And Would Be In Deep Fear. He Would Be Scared As Hell In That Closed Container All Alone, Without You, Without Faith, And Without His Family. It Was Not The Heat Which Bothered Him When He Was Abandoned; It Was Not Hunger Which Bothered Him Then, And Neither Was It Thirst. It Was The Agony Of Being Alone, Being Without His Family, Being In A Strange Place, Being With Strangers Around. And You Have Again Put Him In An Exactly Similar Position."

By now they had reached the expressway and the Range Rover at the toll plaza.

Dr Divya asked the man in the toll about the container, to which he responded that it had crossed some 15/20 minutes back. She estimated that if they drove faster, they could reach them before Nadiad. Pratima too drove her range rover expertly like a jet and shot the car like a bullet on the expressway. It was still early for the busy traffic, but this meant that this would have helped even the container to travel faster. Shortly after half an hour, Pratima overtook the truck with the container, and signaled them to stop. She had pulled her Range Rover slowly in the path of the truck. The truck had to slow down, and within minutes the Scorpio too reached the spot and stopped behind the truck.

The truck belonged to the army, and the driver was utterly pissed-off at the girls in the Range Rover for what they had just done, and then suddenly he heard the loud sounds emanating from the container. He immediately took out the keys to open the door when Kabeer, Meera and Dr Divya stepped out of the Scorpio. Kabeer went to the man seated in the driver's seat and apologized to him. The driver retrieved keys from the dashboard to check the container. Kabeer was trying to explain that it was an emergency when again a loud sound came from the container.

Kabeer ran back towards the door of the container when with a big loud sound, the door cracked and broke open from all the corners. The door fell flat on the Scorpio and shattered the window pane. The top part of the Scorpio was completely crushed, and the height of the SUV was reduced by two feet.

Kabeer with welled eyes full of fear saw Saint, who was bleeding from his head. Before Kabeer could try to get in, Saint jumped at Kabeer and made him fall back on the road. Just then an Innova sped past him, just inches away. Kabeer had got hurt by this fall, and the blood from Saint's forehead dripped on his face. Kabeer started to cry, and hugged Saint tightly, and burst out, "I am so sorry my baby, I am so very sorry. I will never do anything like this again in my entire life. I promise you my *bachcha*. I swear on my lord that I would never ever do it."

Saint was also in tears, he howled loudly, not because of the injury on his head, but because of the emotional reunion with his beloved master. The army man was in a fix now, but he too became emotional, as he understood what had happened. Pratima in a strange mix and match of track pyjama with a shirt; ran with a bowl of water to Saint. Kabeer and Saint moved to one side of the road and drank water from the same bowl in the same manner.

A little laughter broke out from everyone when they saw Kabeer slurping water in Saint's style. Dr Divya took a towel from Shivani which she had fetched from the backseat of her car. She also brought the emergency first-aid box, which was always there in every member of the gang's car. She cleaned up the wound and checked Saint. Luckily the wound was not deep, and not close to the eyes. After she cleaned the wound, she applied betadine lotion, and sprinkled an antiseptic powder to help the blood to clot faster; the bleeding had to stop.

Kabeer apologized to the serviceman, and called up Hridaydeep and narrated the incidence with a lot of apologies. Hridaydeep understood the matter and assured Kabeer not to worry; he would take care of the situation. Hridaydeep called up his brother-in-law in Ladakh, luckily, he understood and accepted the situation, and ordered the serviceman to go back to Ahmedabad.

Meera called-up her office from where the Scorpio was insured and arranged for towing of the vehicle; it was directly sent to the claims section of the service center. All of them got into Pratima's car and drove back. They took the diversion from Nadiad, covered the circle and came back on the expressway towards Ahmedabad. Shivani had called-up Kabeer's home to inform that Saint was with them, though she did not divulge about Saint's injury and the crushed Scorpio.

As soon as they all reached Kabeer's home, Faith was the first one to reach Saint. He was shocked at the injury and started licking it. Dr Divya pointed towards the loving scene of the dogs and told him that that was what love was all about. Faith did not know whether it was a good thing or a bad thing for him to lick the wound, but it really did not matter to him anyway. The doctor wagged her finger at Kabeer, and said in a threatening tone, "Anything you do to him without my knowledge, I swear on your Lord Shiva I will put you in a situation that you will pay with your life for it."

Saint was back where he actually belonged to. Saint got back his friend. Saint got back his buddy. Saint got back his Parents. He got back his entire gang. This was his true habitat; yes Saint had got his habitat.

Saint got his habitat.

The Saint, The Rescue.

The temperature started to drop after the monsoon was over, and Saint had become more active. Now, Saint cherished early morning cold water swims while Kabeer stayed back in the boat. Days were short, but action-packed for Saint. The season of fun festivals had started. First, it was Raksha Bandhan, and Meera tied the sacred thread on both Faith's and Saint's wrists. She got a gold chain as return gift from Kabeer. Kabeer had bought heavy silver chains for both the dogs. Both the chains had a silver plate in the shape of a square with their names on it, and Kabeer's phone number mentioned on the other side. The names inscribed as 'Respected Faith Kapoor' and 'Reverend Saint Kapoor'.

After Raksha Bandhan, it was Ganpati Sthapana when Kabeer had the idol of Lord Ganesha installed in his home for ten days. The idol of Lord Ganesha was of the *bal-swaroop*, where Lord was astride the bull *Nandiji* and held on to the horns of the sacred bull. The aarti was done twice every day, followed by sweet Prashada, made at home. Saint and Faith loved the sweet Prasad very much and always participated in the aarti for the same. Even the turtles, Shubh and Labh, never missed a single aarti, they were brought in the hall every time. Saint spent a lot of time seated in front of the Lord Ganesha idol.

On the first day, Saint had tried to lick Lord Ganesha out of love when Kabeer had stopped him with a strong NO. Saint felt a lot of love for the Lord, while Faith felt a sense of friendship with Lord Ganesha. Faith would either sit next to the idol or would jump and play in front of the idol. Many times he would bring his ball, and try to invite Lord Ganesha to participate like the way he would invite Saint and Kabeer. Every day after the clothes of the idol were changed, Faith would walk to the idol and smell it. On the other hand, Saint stayed very calm in front of the idol, he never jumped around the space where Lord Ganesha was seated. He would sit in front of the Lord, and keep staring at the idol for hours and hours.

Saint was once caught licking the foot of Lord Ganesha's idol, which Kabeer allowed. The night before the day of *Visarjan*, Saint slept next to Lord Ganesha, and in the morning, his head was found placed on Nandiji's chest. There was a lot of discussion among the members of the gang about this, and Dr Divya said that Saint is justifying his name by his divine nature, and his acts. Everyone laughed joyfully, and not in a mocking manner.

After the Ganpati Visarjan, Saint and Faith were little down, but soon it was the *Navratri*. Kabeer and Mummy used to follow the routine of seven days of fasting, and then *Ashtami pooja*. Faith and Saint again had the pleasure of daily *aarti*, and the *prasada*, twice a day. While for the Ganapati Pooja, all the arrangements were taken care of by Kabeer and Meera. The *Navratri's* arrangements were taken care by Mummy and Meera. A table was placed exactly on the spot where Ganpatiji was seated, and it was decorated as per the rituals by Mummy. The *Akhand Diya* was kept lit continuously for nine days.

Faith had a lot of faith in the Navratri festival. Faith hardly moved from the place of the pooja and would sleep under the table on which the Goddess Durga's Sthapna was done. Faith enjoyed and ate only the food prepared, as per the rules, for the fast.

Saint also followed all the pujas and was an active participant of the *aarti*. Saint would swing his head to the tunes of the temple bell and the clapping of the hands. He was the first being to whom the *aarti* was given by Kabeer {*Hands that are warmed by keeping the palms over the flame of the Aarti Diya, and then the warm hands are placed on the other person's head, this is known as giving Aarti*}. Festive time passed by with joy all around. Even Diwali had its share of rituals and lots of sweets, with guests at home, and prayers for everyone. Time actually flew.

It was a holiday, and the entire country was celebrating 26th January, the Republic day. Kabeer had left a little early in the morning with Saint to witness the flag hoisting ceremony in a school. For the family, this was also a big festival. Something that Kabeer missed the most from his school days was the flag hoisting ceremony on Independence Day and Republic Day. Papa was glued to the TV waiting for the PM's speech, and Mummy along with Meera was preparing the special Gujarati breakfast. Kabeer had worn blue Jeans topped with a white shirt. A badge of the Indian flag was pinned on the right chest of his shirt. Saint had been specially groomed in a dog spa just the day before and was adorned with a tricolor scarf around his neck. Kabeer and Saint were going to one of the municipality school to celebrate the great day.

Saint was seated next to Kabeer and was looking out of the window at the passersby, especially the kids in school uniform who marched on the streets. Some carried placards with the theme: 'Respect to Indian Soldiers'. Some others rallied for green environment and reduction of pollution, while few were dressed up like our martyrs Bhagat Singh and Sukhdev.

The car crossed the police ground, where there were some serious activities happening. A huge crowd had gathered to witness the strength of the police system of the city. Kabeer saluted in that direction before entering the lane, which led to the school; he was mesmerized to see a young girl dressed like *Bharat Maa* – 'Mother India'. Few little kids had dressed like M K Gandhi, the father of the Nation. Those innocent faces full of energy made blood flow in Kabeer's veins in a rush of patriotism. He felt more patriotic now than he had ever felt during any India–Pakistan match.

Now the lane got more congested, and some hawkers had gathered outside the school, to sell their home-made delicacies. Some had the masks of the martyrs for sale, and quirky, funny small toys. There were people of all age who roamed in the by lanes and were selling tiny Indian flags that could be stuck on the vehicles and let the flag flutter with the passing wind. It was 8:15 am, and the time scheduled for flag hoisting was 9:00 am. The school was not flush with funds to facilitate the invitation of VIP guests for the ceremony; therefore, the ex-principal was invited to be the chief guest of the function.

Kabeer had parked his car at a place from where he and Saint could clearly see the flag hoisting. Saint was not comfortable in the seat, he wanted to be let out, but Kabeer knew that this could disturb the arrangements made for the ceremony. And if he barked on the road, the solemnity of the situation would be disturbed.

As it is, he had already attracted a lot of attention just by being seated inside the car, even when Kabeer had the window more than half-closed. The chief guest had already arrived and was sitting on the sofa, placed in front of the stage set up, where teachers and students were to perform their acts. The students and the staff had reached the school quite early to ensure that there were no goof-ups during the function. Everybody was on the ground where the national flag was put up to be hoisted.

The flag was filled with flower petals and tied up. There were also some crackers arranged to be burst after the flag was unfurled followed by the national anthem; few girls of the school with sweetest voices were to sing the anthem. Everything was so special, and the involvement of the kids made it much more special for Kabeer and Saint. Even the parents had come to see their kids participating in the program. They were armed with their cameras, and the atmosphere was charged with palpable emotional energy.

Saint was still not comfortable and kept moving restlessly inside the car. He moved from the front seat to the back seat, and vice-versa. Saint was so desperate to step out on the road that he started barking. The more Kabeer tried to cool him down, the more furiously he retaliated. The patriotic songs which were being enjoyed by Saint so far were now drowned by his barks. Kabeer realized that there was too much of a crowd, and he should not have brought Saint along. But now it was too late.

Kabeer observed that the restlessness of Saint was not a usual one; there was a pinch of panic too. Then suddenly Saint jumped, which made the car shake, and it kept shaking for a while. Was it the car which was still shaking because of the Saint's jump or was Kabeer not feeling well because he had skipped breakfast in the morning?

He cleared his mind and realized it was not just the dog or the car that was shaking; everything around him was shaking, from the shop stalls to the ground beneath. Everything started crashing around him. Even inside the school, there was this sudden disturbance, things shook, and the microphone fell to the ground. When the teachers looked around to understand what was happening, they saw that even the chairs, the tables and the stage was shaking tremendously; it was an earthquake. Nature had again chosen 26th January for another calamity.

Panic hit the area, and there was chaos all over. Kabeer immediately started the car to back out from the narrow lane into the open space, but there was so much confusion that it was impossible to move his car even an inch. Kabeer decided to leave the car and walk out from the scanty lane when a sudden loud thud caught his attention. He looked in the direction from the where the sound had come and to Kabeer's shock the weak old buildings were crashing down like a pack of cards.

He immediately tried to get out of his car with Saint held tightly on his leash. He tried to take Saint out, but Saint now refused to get out. The sudden and expected event had not been well judged by Saint, and the loud cries were probably unsettling him. The tremor continued for a minute or so, and then it stopped. By the time the tremors stopped a lot of damage had been done. The main gate of the school had collapsed, and the kids, their parents, and teachers, everyone was stuck inside. Kabeer was worried about Saint, but he was also concerned about the people stuck inside.

He took a deep breath, looked up at the sky, and called his name thrice – "Mahadev, Mahadev, Mahadev" and then sprinted towards the school. There was a high pile of rubble that he had to climb over. He climbed over it with some difficulty, but Saint found it easy to climb because of his expert application of all the four legs. It took half an hour for Kabeer to enter the school with Saint, and by this time another round of tremors had occurred.

Children were scared as hell and were weeping and screaming in fear. He tried to console them, and just then, a teacher drew Kabeer's attention towards a classroom whose roof had collapsed. She mumbled frantically that it was the dressing room, and some kids were stuck in there. Kabeer's horror knew no limits, his throat choked with emotions, and his vision blurred by tears in the eyes.

Meanwhile, Kabeer's family members along with Faith had run out of the house and were seated in their car, parked in an open ground next to the tall buildings; they had carried *Shubh Labh* in a basket. They were continuously making attempts to get in touch with Kabeer but all in vain. Even the telecommunication towers were damaged in the quake. Faith had remained silent, which was a good omen, and they knew that Kabeer was safe. However, Mummy was desperate to hear her son's voice.

Pratima and Shivani were contacted, and they both were safe and sound. Meera could use the internet of her phone, and via the WhatsApp groups, she had confirmed that her family was safe. She told none that Kabeer was not with them. Meera had held a secret which she was yet to share with Kabeer, her heart sank at times. All the residents of the entire building had rushed out earlier. Now, that the quake seemed to have stopped, some of the braver ones headed back home to fetch all their possessions: jewelry and cash.

Papa was completely against this idea, especially as the second tremor had happened much quicker than expected. People were now standing in groups and discussing the disaster. The news spread that the epicenter of the earthquake was *Bhuj*, and it read 6.7 on the Richter scale. Each one prayed for the safety of all.

Kabeer and Saint had by now moved to the collapsed classroom, as Kabeer was moving out and removing the bricks, the screams of the kids stuck inside could be heard, and that struck terror in the hearts of the listeners. Kabeer started to chant the *Maha Mrityunjay mantra*, which gave Kabeer a sense of calmness and required concentration when it was a matter of life and death. Saint was doing his bit of clearing the debris by pushing the stones and rocks away with his hind legs. Looking at them a few male teachers and the chief guest who was the ex-principal also started to help with the rescue work. Somebody shouted from outside the school building that the fire brigade had been called, and should arrive soon.

Kabeer knew it was not a problem that could be solved only by the fire brigade. The challenges were many, and he knew those quite well. Firstly, the lane was too narrow to get the things required for the rescue in. Secondly the entrance to the school was blocked, and it would take quite long to first remove the barriers. Only then would the rescue team be able to reach the kids to save them.

He worried that waiting for so long could prove fatal to the seriously injured ones. They were risking lives here, every moment counted, and every helping hand was important. After removing the bricks and stones, the harsh reality once again stared at them. The concrete blocks of the roof which had fallen were obstructing the kids from escaping, and some were stuck between these blocks. The loud, scared screams of the kids had reduced, and the terror was building around this collapsed building. Kabeer tried hard, but even he could not push the blocks apart. He wandered around trying to find something to help him in his task when his eyes fell on Saint.

Saint was on top of the pile of debris and was trying to push a heavy block with his bare head. Saint had again cut himself probably in the same spot where he was injured before, blood oozed down to his eyes. Despite that he was hard on his task, with a lot of force he managed to push one block away and barked. Kabeer ran and found that there was a boy's bloodied hand visible. The hand was not still, the fingers were moving. However, two heavier blocks were yet to be removed to help the kid out of the debris.

The debris was a pile of hard concrete with twisted and mangled iron rods. Kabeer asked the people in the crowd for a rope, the ex-principal ran towards the flag, and removed the rope from it, and brought it to Kabeer.

Kabeer tied the rope to one of the angled iron and then hooked the loose end of Saint's leash to it. Now Kabeer ran down and started to pull at it, and then instructed Saint to PULL. Saint pulled to the extent his short leash could allow and started to tug hard, the block moved hardly for an inch. Kabeer then shouted once again for Saint to pull hard, and he started to pull with all his might. The concrete block hardly moved, Kabeer ran to the top and saw that the block was stuck behind other block. So, that second block had to be removed first, and then could the main block be removed, but this would take time, and time was something which was not a luxury.

Kabeer ran up and kicked the main block twice in anger, and cursed the block – "FUCK YOU !!!". He then got down, and started to pull the rope tied to the block from a different direction, and instructed Saint to do the same. Kabeer roared ferociously, "HAR HAR MAHADEV" with every pull, and Saint howled too with every pull. The stubborn rock broke yielded, and it moved. As soon as the block moved, some people ran to help Kabeer to pull it; until then he was struggling alone.

That is what hope does to people, it makes them join the movement. The roar of "Har Har Mahadev" got louder as the collective efforts intensified. The block moved out and revealed the head, and shoulder of the boy. Kabeer and a male teacher ran and pulled the boy out with lot of care.

The boy's face was covered completely in blood, and the sight was not for the weak hearted. Saint too ran to the boy and started to lick his face. Seeing this, a person from the ground instructed to move the animal away, "If this animal tastes human blood, then it would go on a killing spree. Keep this animal away from everyone."

Kabeer retaliated with utmost anger in a loud voice, which could be heard far and wide, even at the entrance of the narrow lane, "Just shut the fuck up. If you don't know anything then better keep quiet. Do you know the dog better or I? It was this bloody dog or your ancestors who initiated to save this boy? One more word which hinders what we are trying to do and you will curse yourself for being blessed with the ability to speak." The man, whom Kabeer was addressing, began to tremble in absolute fear, and he slowly sat down on the floor with his legs folded, and his head bent low stuck to his chest.

Kabeer turned towards the boy, the face was by now licked clean. He began to regain consciousness. A cut on the forehead near the eyes was revealed as the source of the oozing blood. Immediately a lady teacher tore a piece of her *chunni* (the long scarf worn around the neck) and tied the wound tight to stop the bleeding. Kabeer ran back to the rescue spot and looked inside; there were many more kids who were still stuck there.

Some parts of their body were visible, while mostly they seemed to be stuck under the collapsed roof. By now, few journalists had reached the other side of the school's blocked entrance and were frantically recording the happenings from different angles at the height of survived apartments.

It was hard luck that the collapsed roof was hindering them from going in. One of the journalist shouted that the fire brigade had reached the lane, but was not able to enter as there was one more building which had collapsed at the entrance of the lane. There were more people stuck under that building.

First, they were being rescued, only then they would come to the school for rescue work.

Kabeer was in total confusion as what he had to do now, and then he spotted Saint on the extreme right side of the collapsed classroom. He was rapidly moving the stones with his powerful forelegs. Kabeer ran and joined him, and a few others followed him. Saint had uncovered a small foot of a girl wearing an anklet. Kabeer immediately started to move the bricks and stones, one leg of the girl was visible, and it was clad in a saree wrapped in a traditional way. The lady teacher saw the leg, gasped, and fell unconscious. The girl who was stuck was her daughter, who had to play the role of Bharat Maa.

Kabeer removed as many pieces as possible and was successful in clearing quite a bit. The clearing made a cave-like thing where the big almost 5 feet by 4 feet concrete block was above the body, but it hung on another rock and had not fallen on the body.

This big concrete block was almost two feet away from the girl, and a lot of small pieces of the concrete covered her. He had by now got all the small pieces out, and the girl up to her waist could be seen in the light. Kabeer crawled in to inspect, and he was able to gauge that the girl's head was injury free and that the girl was lying upside down with her hands extended out. He crawled out and suggested others to slowly pull out the girl. They tried to do it, but found it futile; probably she was pinned somewhere by a block.

Kabeer once again crawled in and tried to check. Unfortunately, thc girl's hand was buried under a big piece of concrete. Though the block was not heavy, on top of it was a bigger piece of concrete block. Unless the big block was not removed first, it was nearly impossible to rescue the little girl.

Kabeer again crawled in and tried to push the big block upward, but nothing happened. The block surely weighed above a hundred kilos. He spoke to Saint, and rubbed his neck, then directed him to crawl under the big block. Saint's structure was much bigger compared to that of Kabeer's, and he found it difficult to enter, yet he kept at it and managed to push himself in.

He could barely get his body a little more than his shoulders in. The girl's body was now between his legs. Kabeer then instructed Saint to get up and to push the block up. Kabeer kept saying in an encouraging manner, "Come on my boy, get up. Get up my boy, you can do it, yes… Come on! Push the rock! Come on push the rock!" Saint started to push it like he was doing the push-ups, and the rock moved a little. Immediately Kabeer caught the girl's legs and asked Saint to push further up.

All the while, Kabeer kept throwing instructions at Saint. Saint now began to howl and started to bark. Finally, with a very loud howl he lifted the rock by almost two inches, which allowed Kabeer to pull the girl out, and everybody cheered loudly and clapped happily. However, Kabeer's focus was now on the next move. He immediately placed another big rock below the mega block lifted by Saint. He placed it in such a way that the lifted block rested on the rock. This allowed Saint to ease his body down, and to crawl out.

Saint's back was bruised, hair scrapped off his body, and deep blood oozing scratches were all over his body. Though he was bleeding profusely, he was happy to help one of the human species which had abandoned him at one time.

On the other side of the river Sabarmati, where Kabeer lived, the constructed buildings were better and much stronger. Life had almost resumed to normalcy by now, though the fear and threat of aftershocks prevailed among the residents. People were glued to the TV, and the news channels kept updating every few minutes, and live reports kept streaming in. In one of the channels, Saint's rescue efforts were being telecasted.

Saint was too tired, but still, he kept at the rescue effort. He sniffed the room to see if there were more lives to be saved. He put his own life at stake. There was blood dripping from his forehead, his entire back was bruised badly, but he was a dog on a mission. Then suddenly somebody shouted the welcome news, "By the grace of Allah, the rescue team has arrived.", and the crowd started to chant, "Allah Hu Akbar, Allah Hu Akbar."

Kabeer waited to understand as what was happening because the biggest blockage of the collapsed wall at the gate had cut the school form the rest of the area. It did not even allow the view of the other side. It was only the shouts which could communicate. After almost ten minutes of waiting when Kabeer could not sense any movement he shouted, "What's the scene? For God's sake do something."

A reply came back, "The blockage is severe, and our machines can cut through concrete only about a foot. This blockage is more than five feet in width; it can't be cut and has to be removed. Only then can we come into rescue." This was from the head of the rescue team at the main gate of the school.

Kabeer shouted back, "Tell us how to move it, we find it almost impossible to move even the big, flat concrete blocks inside. This blockage at the gate looks like a mountain to be moved."

Someone else replied, "If we all move the block inside, then it will be comparatively easier, because the road is at height, and it tilts towards the school. If all who are outside push together, and the ones inside pull simultaneously, then there is some possibility. Apart from that, we will have to wait till the special rescue teams from the other countries come-in."

Another person from outside contributed, "Allah bless all, but the fact is that other cities closer to the Kutch are more devastated by the impact of the shivering earth, and all such help will be provided to them first. We have to manage this on our own."

Kabeer shouted back, "Then in the name of Lord Rudra, Let us do it. Throw us the ropes." Lot of ropes were thrown in with a lot of difficulty and multiple attempts. It took almost an hour for the people inside to hook the ropes to the broken rocks and concrete blocks at the entrance. Outside the people had brought the logs of fallen trees, and were ready to push as hard as possible. It was decided that one of the journalists would do the counting into his microphone, and on the count of three, the people outside would hit the blockage with the tree logs, and at the same time those inside, would pull. Saint was in the center leading the small force of men. A few had lost hopes, but what mattered was that the remaining few still had their hopes high.

"One", "Two", "Three", and the atmosphere echoed with Allah Hu Akbar, and the block was hit hard simultaneously with the roars of HAR HAR MAHADEV and Saint's howls the men inside the school pulled the ropes. After an hour of pushing and pulling, loud rounds of praising Mahadev and Allah by human voices, the incredible howling of a dog, the largest block moved a foot inside, and the emptied space filled up with small blocks.

Now the push from outside broke the small blocks but was not effective in pushing the biggest block at all. It was quite certain that if they were able to move the big block out of the way, then things could be immediately sorted out. That would allow an entire passage to be made for the rescue team to enter. Finally, one of the active persons inside decided to try for it till their death.

This attitude inspired even those without hopes; all had joined in for the common cause. Every unit of strength was useful. Saint again was in the middle, and the others were on either side of him. They tried to pull the block, but they slipped and fell down. Once again, they repeated their action. Their hands also slipped from the rope, and that scrapped the skin of their hands. This time nobody gave up, and after 35 to 40 minutes, the block surrendered to the will of these determined rescuers, and by the grace of God, it moved out of the passage.

Family members ran in to meet their beloved ones. Meera, Papa and Faith also ran in. The rescue team got down to their task immediately, and they started to cut the concrete blocks carefully to avoid injuring anybody stuck in there. Faith whined and licked Saint's wounds, as he lay on the ground breathing heavily. Meera had already given water to Saint, which he drank slowly, and intermittently. The doctors who had come along with the rescue team attended Saint also.

Rescue continued for another five hours till every possible rescue was made. Unfortunately, they unearthed a few dead bodies, although fortunately quite a few lives were saved. It got dark soon, and the team was about to announce that the rescue work is over, when two sets of parents came in crying and informed that their kids were still missing, and could be still alive.

Immediately, bright torches were lit-up to search, but no one was found. The rescue team decided to break all the concrete as the last attempt, but Kabeer stopped them as this would end the life with some sudden fall of concrete on the still alive kids He turned to Faith and asked him to go in and sniff.

Faith was not a professionally trained sniffer but was surely better than humans. Kabeer made Faith run to the rescued kids, made him sniff them, and then back to the concrete mess, and started to yell, "Fetch it, baby, fetch it." It took some time for Faith to understand what exactly Kabeer wanted him to do, and as soon as he understood he got into action.

Being a mix-Labrador Faith was lean in size and was able to move into places, where even light could not reach. There was a fear of Faith getting stuck, but he was no less a brave heart philanthropist than his own master and friend. After about fifteen minutes, he stood near the collapsed bathroom, which was adjacent to the damaged classroom, and started to bark. Bingo, he had found at least one.

He wriggled back, and the rescue team with equal diligence started to cut the concrete and finally found the head of a boy with a skull cap worn by the Muslims. Of the unfound two, the elder one, a 5th Standard student–Iqbal – was spotted. Rescue team kept on cutting in circles and pulled out the limp body of the boy. Just below him, almost in his cuddle was the younger boy, a Sr. KG student–Rajeev who started crying. He, too, was pulled out very gently.

Tragically, the older boy had died due to an internal injury when a concrete block had fallen on him. He had covered and protected the younger boy from harm with his own body, and thereby saved his life.

The atmosphere was charged with mixed emotions. The announcement was finally made that the rescue work was completed. Everyone went back to their homes. The next day every television channel was full of reports about the rescue miracles. They mentioned the heroes, including defense people who were a major part of the effort.

Kabeer had a constant smile on his face from the moment he had retired the previous day. Saint was also shown as one of the Heroes, he was. And not far away, somewhere, the master who had abandoned him was also seeing and crying for his karma.

Saint had been once again shaved off for his treatment by Dr Divya.

One of the journalists from the local newspaper, who had been regularly publishing reports that were against pets and stray animals, had landed up in Kabeer's house that evening. He interviewed Kabeer about Saint, and it was then revealed that Saint happened to be the same dog which was rescued six months back. That story made headlines in all the television channels and the newspapers. "A DOG RESCUED SIX MONTHS BACK, PAYS BACK TO HUMANITY BY RESCUING HUMANS: WHEN WILL HUMANS LEARN THAT?"

It is said that the world is round, and life always takes a full circle. For Saint, it had happened within a short span of six months. From him being rescued as an abandoned dog and being rehomed, to him rescuing others. There were two words to define the giant dog that looked like a lion: 'Saint' and 'Rescue.'

Yes.

The Saint. The Rescue.

Epilogue

Dr Divya had for the first time wept like a kid, hugging Saint. She was almost wailing, and it took efforts from Meera to console her. Saint was in a worse condition when he was rescued, but even then, Dr Divya had not cried. Neither Dr Divya had any emotional experiences with Saint to make her cry that day. Then Pratima and Shivani made her swear on their gang to spill the beans, and she opened up.

Very early in her career, she was once bitten by a Saint Bernard. It was a hot summer day, and the dog was in a terrible mood, there was no mistake on the dog's part as even in summers he was without any cooling conditions and hence was thoroughly irritated. Due to this terrible incident, she had stopped treating Saint Bernards as a rule. However, with the passage of time, she learnt that her decision was wrong. However, since that realization, she never had the opportunity to treat a Saint Bernard as a patient.

So when she saw Saint abandoned, she wanted him to be rescued and wanted to take him on as her patient. She had purposefully revisited the abandoned Saint next day instead of the evening; so that it gave Kabeer that extra time he needed to rescue Saint.

After Saint's rescue, the second shock she had got was when Saint was being sent off to Ladakh. The thought of losing Saint was the reason she had bashed Kabeer, and she was not at all sorry for that. What Saint had done now was truly heroic and beyond her wildest imagination. If something had happened to Saint during this rescue, then she would have been unimaginably miserable. Kabeer heard her out and patted her lightly, but he still had his constant smile. When everyone was feeling bad for Divya, Kabeer kept smiling mysteriously.

Pratima hugged Dr Divya, and then she announced, "Guys finally my parents' hearts have melted after they heard about the heroic acts of Saint. They have agreed to allow me to bring home a pet dog, my own baby." To this, Kabeer gave Pratima a side hug and kept smiling mysteriously.

When everyone got busy opening up their hearts and sharing their joys, Kabeer too opened up and began to explain the reason of his inscrutable smiles. Meera had broken the news to him the previous night; she was pregnant. Kabeer was to become a father soon. Saint had brought so much happiness in one way or the other to every life he had touched.

Other Books

an ancient tool to Law of Attraction
BEST SELLER
The Science of Mantras
DARPAN GOYAL

IF LOVE HAD MORE NAMES
PAIN
FREEDOM
REVENGE
FEAR
SEX
GREED
DARPAN GOYAL

If Love had more names.

(Sample)

Why didn't you wait?

It was a hot afternoon, and school was over for the day. A boy of the eleventh standard, with his handkerchief wrapped around his palm in style, and necktie hung loose on his shirt he was styling his hair in the side view mirror of his bike when his third girlfriend of the year came running to him.

"Did you hear?" She asked him excitedly.

"What?" He had cigarette pressed to his lips, unlit.

"*Arre*, Dr R. K Arora is coming to deliver a lecture at our school." A backpack hung on one shoulder, top two buttons of the shirt open, and while chewing gum, she was searching the pocket of her short uniform skirt, for the matchbox.

"That *to,* I know. Even the poster is ready to be put on the notice board. But what's so exciting about it? We have plenty of such shitty guests every year, trying to thrust their ideologies on us. Which are so bookish that I doubt if they ever practice the same in their own lives." He animated exhaling the smoke from the unlit cigarette.

"To hell with their fuckin' ideologies." She pulled the cigarette from his fingers and lit it. "You are just not gettin' it." She blew the smoke in rings on his face and handed over the cigarette to him.

"Not getting what…?" He now wanted to know exactly what she was trying to convey.

"Dr, R K Arora means Rati Arora – 'The Rati Arora'." Last three words were spoken with a pause emphasizing each one.

"What the fuck?" He couldn't believe it, "You mean the Rati-Krunal *wali* Rati?" He even forgot to smoke his cigarette.

"Yes, you bugger. The Rati-Krunal, on whom, you keep swearing for your love." She took the cigarette from his hands and walked out. Rati-Krunal needed no introduction to that school.

The love story of Rati and Krunal had started and ended three decades ago. Year after year, and batches after batches, Rati and Krunal were still the icons or rather the Gods of love, especially for the school.

Everyone in the school used to swear by their love.

***

Finally, the day came.

It was a bright morning of the most awaited Sunday. The school had never witnessed a hundred percent 'attendance' ever, except for the exams. The strength of parents, along with their children superseded the count of any parent-teacher meeting. It was not the activity, but the guest, everyone wanted to know about. Dr R K Arora, an alumnus of the same school, was one of the invited guests. The function was coming to a close, and the host, a boy of the senior-most batch, announced.

"The wait is over. Time has come to give rest to our perspiring hearts and have the woman on stage who has been acclaimed for her work in the field of cardiac surgeries say it as 'dealing with hearts,' by the whole world. But her name resides in the heart of this very school."

The boy continued, "Everyone's heart beats for self, but if your heart beats for someone special, then this is the lady you want to see and hear from. Overwhelmed to announce her name, please welcome Dr R K Arora."

A lady in her late forties walked up the dais. Dark tan eyes, dense hair in a traditional braid, high cheekbones, sharp jawline with pink complexion. The only thing which was out of place was the colour of her Patiala dress. It was pale white, without a hint of any other color. She spoke in her deep husky voice.

"Hello, everyone."

And the crowd was silent; no one wanted to disturb the aura of her words. All they wanted was to hear her, but she didn't have much to say; she was a person of few words. After a brief formal speech, she opened the platform for question and answer session. For a couple of minutes, there was a pin-drop silence that was broken by a girl of the eleventh standard.

"Mam, you are a name which is known to every student of this school. Be it an old student like me with over a decade of tenure, or a recent joinee of few days, everyone knows what 'Rati and Krunal' mean for the lovers." There was loud cheer at the mention of Rait-Krunal, together. The cheer was louder than the previous one when she was invited to speak. Without Krunal, even Dr R K Arora sounded incomplete. Once the noise was settled, she continued. "But at the same time, no one knows the story of 'Rati and Krunal'. I ask you for that story."

Pearled tears curtained Rati's eyes, and the sweetest of a smile with a pinch of sorrow drew on her face. She spoke nothing, but she could recall everything as if she was still living in that era; the era of 1980s.

That time her school was the only English medium school in the city. One of a kind where boys shared seats with girls in the classroom, they were supposed to sit roll number wise. While her name on the register was Joshi Rati, he was registered as Krunal Arora; roll number 27 and 28 respectively. He didn't know Gujarati, and she found Punjabi phrases witty; that was the ice breaker, and in no time they were the best of pals. Recess was the only time they could spend chit-chatting, there were no WhatsApp, facebook or mobile phones to communicate; he didn't even have a landline at home.

The lesser the time, the more valuable it became. They cherished those eighteen minutes of recess for the rest of eighteen hours spent apart. By the end of the year, their friendship grew-up to love, and whispers of their relationship were getting louder. They were nearing the end of the session that was to be followed by a two months' break. He was scheduled to spend entire vacation at his grandparents' place in Ferozpur, Punjab. But instead of cribbing over the distance, they relished each moment in a way that they could walk over those sixty days just by recalling those memories.

One fine day, a week before the vacation to break, Rati asked Krunal, "Can you come to my home in the evening? My parents are to attend a marriage, and we will have hours at our disposal." He agreed on the same instance. To make it memorable, he bought a blank audio cassette and carried his 'Walkman' to record their conversations. He couldn't think of a thing better than that, he would take her voice with him to Punjab.

He was now at the doors, with nervous hands, he rang the bell; she opened the door and found him blushing like a bride with a rose flower in his hand. Krunal had never seen her before in a salwar suit; she looked grown-up. He pushed the button to start recording the conversation from the moment he stepped in. It was his first visit to her home; he was the first boy to visit her home. It was a special moment and demanded to be treated that way; she had prepared tea for the first time in her life.

The passion of romance was at its peak. They were seated opposite to each other on the sofa, in the crossed-leg postures, holding each other's hands; yes, for the first time. Unexpectedly, the doorbell rang; she could recognize the voice. "Daddy!" she exclaimed. She had heard the buzzer of the lift, but she wasn't anticipating their return so early. She immediately checked the time on the cuckoo wall clock, she was right, they were two hours early.

None of them knew what to do, their minds were clogged. Every attempt to think of an excuse for Krunal's presence was futile; a boy had never been allowed to come home even in the parents' presence. It took some time for the love birds to realise that there was no option but to face the wrath.

Krunal was mentally prepared even for a bashing. What he feared was if the news reaches his abode, he could be deported to Punjab forever. The thought of being separated from Rati brought tears rolling down his face. By now, the doorbell was heard repeatedly, and the door banged hard. With shivering hands and quivering body, she opened the door.

At first sight, her parents sighed relief to see their daughter safe, but as soon as their eyes settled on the boy, the situation turned into a tornado. A couple of slaps on her face and few kicks to the boy was just the start. Harshness was not in their actions but in their words. Rage multiplied with every passing second and in no time, chide turned into abuses, and then into allegations; allegations on Rati's character.

Rati could not believe what her father was speaking for her and her character. She had never even heard anyone say such things to anyone, except in movies. She couldn't stand it and burst into tears. But that was not the end, at the helm of her mental weakness thronged by his curses, a sentence erupted from her father's mouth, "It would have been better to see you dead instead."

Her weeping stopped abruptly, she looked at her mom, who turned away her face in dismay. Rati too turned around, with tear flooded eyes she said, "I love you, Krunal." She meant what she said, and she did say it for the last time. She sprinted towards the balcony and jumped off the ninth floor. Krunal rushed, her parents ran, but the damage was done. She had fallen on the pointed spokes of the wooden railing that separated the road from the garden of the society. Her blood dripped on the petals of a rose, the color did not have much of a difference.

Rati's parents panicked for the lift, whilst Krunal shot downstairs. A crowd had already gathered, and ambulance was called by the society residents. With the help of few men, Krunal managed to pull her out, stabbed, from the pointed railing. She wasn't breathing but was profusely bleeding. He came closer to her and whispered his last words; "How could you even think that you can leave me alone? I will be there before you..." and he left from that place.

The Walkman in his pocket automatically click stopped; batteries were out, the charge was gone, there wasn't any life left.

By evening there were two news stories making rounds across the streets of the city. **'A boy poisoned himself to death, he was in love.'** And **'A girl miraculously escaped from the jaws of death, the reason could only be love.'**

It took some days for Rati to recover, and the news of Krunal's death was shared with her along with an audio cassette; it had every word spoken on that evening.

Even three decades later, the echoes of those words made a tear dodge her eyes. The principal shook her to bring her to the present. She was still standing on the dais, and entire school waiting for her story. Rati this time faked a smile and said, "I really don't think that my story carries any relevance today, but one learning I have which surely is relevant. If you want, I can share that."

There was no answer from the crowd; her long silence ending in a tear had created a lump in everyone's throat. Finally, the principal of the school squeezed Rati's hands and nodded in affirmation. With a belief, how great her love story must be, everyone knew how important learning would be.

Rati spokc, "I am the widow of Krunal Arora, the man I loved but could not marry." There was a wave of aghast in the crowed. Without revealing much, she had told what made 'Rati-Krunal' the Gods of love.

"It was Krunal's demise that made me realise how it feels when we lose someone we love. I will never give that kind of a pain to anyone; I know how it feels.

A real love; be it a successful or a failed one; honored or cheated; lived or played, but can never be the reason for the end of life." She dropped her eyeshades and left immediately, her eyes could not control anymore.

In a few hours, she was with her parents and listening to the same audio for the third consecutive time. Finally, when her father didn't allow her to play it again, she questioned him.

"Why didn't you wait? You could have heard me once before putting up those allegations."

"Why didn't you wait? My anger would have calmed down after sometime; you could have told me everything instead of jumping off." He countered in same anguish.

"Why didn't you wait?" She looked up towards the sky, "You could have at least waited till my last breath before ending your life." and she wailed her guts out.

The Science of Mantras

(Sample)

The most powerful Mantra

Vyom was still engrossed in the discussion he had been through. He shared and discussed the same with Meenakshi too, and her reaction was an emulation of his. They were stunned to learn the way Mantras have been misunderstood. *Mahamrityunjaya* Mantra was one of the most popular Mantra, and if people were unaware of it then, it was scary to think of those Mantras which were lesser known and prescribed as remedies.

He decided to decipher the *Gayatri* Mantra similarly. He had to comprehend his favorite Mantra. He played with his turtles for a very long time and slumbered when felt completely drained. He used to play like this when they were young, but it was more enjoyable when they had grown-up and were more active. They would also have enjoyed, as such games were reminders of their own childhood.

Next day, he continued with the awareness mediation and reached office well before time. He had not checked his cell phone and neither his mails. He opted for a search engine and typed 'word by word meaning of Gayatri Mantra', surfed lot of sites to get to the unbiased meaning of the Mantra. One thing was common in all sites, before the meaning there was information about the purpose of it and a luring one.

Soon it was time for the office, and his team members came in, and he got busy with the schedule. That day he winded-up with the closing hours of the office and went straight home. It took him two more days of similar schedule before he had the complete description of *Gayatri* Mantra. Well in time to take the material Ahmedabad for a discussion with his better half.

The discussion was held on a post-dinner walk and crested in the garden.

"So, are you done with your study of the Mantra?" Meenakshi initiated the discussion directly from the topic, she was quite curious to know.

"Yes. It is a wonderful Mantra, where most of it comprises of praises to God and seeks nothing more than the direction for the mental faculties."

"That is interesting. So, there are some Mantras which are not scripted for just materialistic consumption."

"Yes, and the reason is that these Mantras were not encrypted in today's times."

"I think it's too harsh. Even today, most of the humans are not selfish, and do a lot of things just for their mental solace."

"I am not sure of this. But you have the right to stick to your opinion."

"I have a solid platform, as a base to my opinion. I have been following a blog, namely humanityinthecity.com, and there are articles on real-life incidences where people have felt humanity. I also know a couple who spend a lot of time with dogs on the streets. They have a pet dog, and still, they feel for those on the streets. You can't call this as materialistic one."

"Ahan, this is nice. But let's get back to our discussion on *Gayatri* Mantra."

"Yes, please continue. I am eager to learn about it."

"It starts with *Om.*"

"Yes, and *Om* is not a part of the mantra, but a sound prefixed to every Mantra. Now go ahead with the Mantra, dear."

"The first word is *Bhur,* it implies existence. God is self-existent and independent of all. God is eternal and unchanging, without a beginning and without an end. God exists as a continuous, permanent and a constant entity. Another meaning of the word *Bhur* is earth, on which we are born and sustained. Earth provides us everything we need. So, in this context, we can call earth also as a form of God only."

"This is quite interesting; we never acknowledged the importance of earth like a God." Meenakshi amused.

"You are right, as Manish would have quoted; we lack awareness. God is the source of all, and it is through HIS divine will that all of us are blessed with all that we require to maintain us through our lives. For that matter, to a large extent, we can say it for the earth too, it provides us with everything required to maintain us."

"What about the air? Earth does not provide us with air to breathe?"

"May not be directly, but it is through trees and plants, that we get the required Oxygen. Without earth, none of the greenery could have prevailed, hence no air too." Vyom clarified.

"That's another important point. Not only for earth but in many other things too, we acknowledge only what we can observe as a direct offering. We forget that lot of things are offered to us after being processed at many stages, and this should not dilute the contribution of the one who offered the first raw input to have us the final product."

"Very much like farmers who are hardly given their credit, monetarily and non-monetarily."

"You are absolutely right."

"There is a third interpretation also of the word *Bhur,* referring to *Prana* literal meaning is 'life' but implied meaning is 'breath' or the 'air' we breathe."

"Hmm…So, here the importance of air is directly acknowledged too."

"Not only acknowledged darling but given the prominence like that of a God.

God is the one who gives life to all. Whilst HE is independent of all, all are dependent on HIM. It is God only who has given us life, maintains us throughout our lives, and solely can take it away too, whenever HE chooses to. That's what the word *Bhur* means."

"Vyom, if just a single word has made filled us with gratitude, what would be the impact of the whole mantra? No doubt, you feel tranquil while chanting it."

"Well, that's why it is a science. I used to feel so better when I didn't know the meaning, now with meaning the effect would be manifold higher."

"Go ahead with the rest of it too."

"Oh! Yes. The next is *Bhuva,* meaning consciousness, the consciousness of self and everything else. It covers the principle which Manish quoted as awareness. Consciousness/awareness empowers you to control each and everything. Though, some scholars read the word *Bhuva* for 'greatness'."

"Greatness? This is altogether different from consciousness."

"In a way, it is different, but if we see from another angle, it coincides with consciousness. At a high level of consciousness, you gain the ability to control things, and that is the greatness of it. You increase the goodness and diminish the bad. And through your control, you multiply the happiness and remove all the sorrow and pain."

"I feel here we should include the mind part also. As it is said, it is not the situation but your response to the situation which creates happiness or sorrow." The insight came from Meenakshi.

"To some extent, I agree with it. But there are situations like death when you simply cannot choose to be happy. The pain and sorrow in this and other similar situations are inevitable."

"I agree on Vyom. But death is something which is a fragment of nature; none can be immortal, right? And neither is this Mantra allied to anything with death. Let death be treated like a Sunset. The grief and pain is inevitable, but for how long? You will miss the presence of the person you have lost, but does that mean you lose all the rights to be happy too. Does the death of one person defy the existence of others who are so vital in your life?"

"What are you trying to say? I know you are the right person to talk about it; you have recently lost someone you were so close to. But, removal of sorrow and pain in such a condition doesn't seem to be plausible."

"Take it this way. You cannot fill the void of life, but you have a choice to stick to that void and be in pain or stick to those who are still there and be happy for their being in your life. If I lose an eye, I lose an eye; but I still have another eye to see, and that is something fascinating and to be happy about. Whenever I think about the lost sight, I will be down and drowned but whenever I think of the other one I will feel blessed, and there would be nothing to stop that smile on my face.

By being conscious, I control my thought process and choose to focus on what I have, hence choose to be happy. Got it?"

"Got it. When it comes to death we should be more accepting for the event. And instead of trying to control the event, we should control our response to the event and make a conscious decision of being happy about what we have." concluded Vyom.

"Right. I am now able to understand why Manish said that awareness is a non-negotiable pre-requisite. It all starts with being aware of ourselves and everything around us. Well, what's the next word in the Mantra?"

"*Swah,* and it connotes omnipresence. God is omnipresent and being formless it becomes plausible. The formless can take up any form and be present anywhere. With this the first part of the four parts Mantra completes."

"So, in the first quarter of the Mantra, we converse about the various and majestic qualities of God and also express gratitude towards earth and air as God. We not only praise the *Bhur* facet of God but also try to adapt the 'consciousness' as a facet of ours too."

"Yes. The second quarter is *Tatsavitur Varenyam.* Here *Tat* stands for 'that', it is more of a pointer or indicator referring to God. And the word which comes next is the soul of the Mantra, and God is referred to as 'that' *Savitur.*"

"Oh, I always believed that *tatsa* is a word and *vitur* is another word. Don't you think that we have been too ignorant, to be called educated? We learnt so many things and technicalities commissioning hell of projects and assignments, but obliviously by-passed to understand a Mantra. Not just a Mantra but The Mantra, the Mantra which we have been chanting so often."

"You still had an impression about it, even if a false one. I had not even bothered to ponder if there are words or not. Like the trait of a parrot, I would repeat the Mantra 108 times, and that was all I did. Anyways, it's never too late."

"Yeah, it is never too late. So, now tell me about *Savitur*, the soul of the Mantra."

"*Savitur* means creation. God is the supreme creator and identified as a divine bright luminous light, like that of a Sun. Sun too is mentioned here like a God."

"It has to be, it is as indispensable as earth and air. Importance of sunrays has gained so much popularity with science too. There are so many diseases which are cured by the sunlight."

"You are right, and as we discuss, I have noted one more thing about both the Mantras we deciphered."

"What?"

"There is not even a single word in the Mantras, which is negative in nature like ailment or agony."

"But we discussed the sorrow part? And it came from the discussion of one of the parts of the *Gayatri* Mantra itself."

"We discussed it because *Bhur* implies the removal of sorrow. But it means consciousness, and with the consciousness, we remove sorrow and pain."

"Ok. But what is the point you are drawing?"

"It means that negativity is a non-existing artifice. Only positivity exists like vigor and bliss. Death is also not considered negative here. The negativity like ailment and grief is absence of vigor and bliss. Just like darkness is the absence of light and there is no veracity of darkness as such."

"But we can also say that light is the absence of darkness, well-being is the absence of ailment and glee is the absence of distress or agony."

"You can say that I can say that and anyone can say that. But Mantras do not say that it is the theme in which the Mantras are coded, the theme of positivity. And going with the same philosophy even death is the accomplishment of life and not the end. When a life completes, another initiates, through the cycle of reincarnation/ rebirth. And if the cycle is totally complete, the life destines for Moksha."

"This angle is quite interesting. How did it strike you? This is too brilliant to be noticed by you…" she laughed playfully.

"Now you are underestimating a genius here.

To be honest, the meaning of *Savitur* struck this thought to me. *Savitur* means creation and is the soul of this Mantra, which means obliteration has no place at all. What we perceive as destruction is actually the triumph, triumph in a role and time to move on to the next role. Like a promotion, when we get promoted as a Manager it does not mean that our previous role has been destroyed or ended. It just means that we have successfully concluded that role and now is the time for another role."

"And what is your opinion about those who get fired?"

"That simply means that they were playing the role wrong or the role erroneously, and they are given a new role by some other company or through a completely new profession."

"Isn't it the demeaning way of providing a new role? By being fired from your work or to take up a lower role in some other company/industry/profession?"

"I won't say that; no role can ever be demeaning. Lord Krishna took up the role of a driver for Arjun, was he demeaning himself? Or was Arjun demeaning the Lord by accepting him as his driver?

"Hmm... This is another intelligent argument from you."

"Thank You. But, at the given moment, you need to play a role, and it could be different from the role you are used to. Who knows, tomorrow you might leave this job or are forced to leave this job and take-up something new. This in the starting might not appeal to you, but in the future, may work out to be a blessing. You have heard the phrase – blessing in disguise."

"This is a crazy thought, but the example makes it sound sensible."

"It is a sensible thought. Even the word *Savitur* mentions the power of creation and creativity. It covers all, from the arts like drawing, craft, dance or music going to the scientific inventions and discoveries, and also the creation of another life as a newborn baby."

"That means like the earth, the air and the sun, we humans are also God?"

"We undoubtedly are creators, and God is the supreme creator. As he created the ones, who can further create. The creation part is of such importance that the *Gayatri* Mantra is also known as *Savitri* Mantra."

"This is so deep. It feels like an entire series could be published with Mantras as a topic. Every word goes so deep, and the best part is that the depth is like an ocean. Man cannot fathom the depth but can go as deep as he wishes to; similarly, the meaning of each word in the Mantra and the entire Mantra is so deep that we can keep on taking plunges to the extent we wish to. Now tell me about *Varenyam.*"

"*Varenyam* means the one 'who is worthy'. God is the only one worthy of being followed and attained. There is a mention that whatever we attain or achieve in life gives us pleasure for some time only. When time passes, our pleasure reduces and eventually diminishes. But if we attain God, that happiness remains forever unaffected."

"That is the biggest question, my dear genius. What is the meaning of attaining God?"

"So far what I have understood through Mantras is that through the characteristics of God, a particular lifestyle has been inscribed with various features. To be positive and creative is one, Gratitude is another. Equating God with earth, air and sun, as the ones to provide us with everything we require fragmented and nourished growth is to develop a sense of responsibility and gratitude towards it. Discussion of death, in the light of consciousness, as a pass-way to Moksha, is again to empower ourselves to control happiness and health. If we follow these things and keep chanting the Mantras as a tool of constant reminders and autosuggestions for the conscious mind, we will attain God. So, my view is when you reach a stage where no such reminders and autosuggestions are required, and you live a happy, healthy life, you have attained God."

"Are you denying God's existence as an entity?"

"Yes. I am saying that there is no entity as God, neither energy nor a power. But at the same time I am voicing that God is all these things. We discussed a while before, by being formless God makes his presence in every form. Similarly, by not being anything, God becomes everything. And Mantras tell us how to be a part of everything."

"It's always complicated when it comes to God."

"Then leave the discussion on God. Maybe later we would be educated enough to discuss this topic. Let's just follow what sinks in. Creativity does? Happiness does? Health does? Consciousness does?..."

"Yes, yes baba. Got it. Precisely identified by you, maybe we are yet to be educated to that degree to discuss and understand God like a kindergarten student cannot understand aerospace. But we are educated enough to understand and decipher Mantras. So, let's do that as of now."

"Fine, as you say. Let us carry on with the third section of the Mantra *Bhargo Devasya Dhimahi.*

Bhargo means purity, God is absolutely pure and his characteristic of making others pure. It signifies the glorious light, which actually is God's love and power."

"This sounds so soothing. You know if I close my eyes and utter *Bhargo,* I can actually visualize that glorious light purifying me."

"You should feel that" he commented in a playful taunt, "Because sinners need it."

"Shut-up. In fact, that way you liar salespeople, need it the most," she retaliated playfully.

"Here also the point I made some time back is reiterated. Purification happens by destroying all sins and afflictions. It could have been directly mentioned here, but it isn't. Do you know why?"

"I got your point. Because it has a negative base and Mantras have been authored in a complete positive perspective. Now go on with the Mantra."

"Good, so you are now grasping it quick. The next word in the *Gayatri* Mantra is *Devasya,* meaning *devata,* i.e. *devas* & *devis.* Though this sounds very routine; mention of *devas* & *devis* in a Mantra, but the explanation makes it quite interesting. It mentions a state where all *devas* and *devis* combine in one."

"Why, combine in one?"

"If you realise *devas* are actually different but divine aspects and characteristics of one God only. Unison of all *devas* means God in completeness, this again refers to the formless God. As all *devas* are in different forms, but when they are together in unison, when they become one, God becomes formless."

"Formless, no form and hence present in every form. It is so wonderfully mentioned."

"So, true. Next is *Dhimahi* – which means to meditate on HIM, using our intellect which is the literal translation of *Dhi.* Here we make a communiqué that 'I meditate on God only, through my intellect and I attempt to become like that one' while communicating to become like HIM, we should think about all the discussed characteristics."

"Here, again comes the imagination into place. While meditating, we actually salute to God remembering all the characteristics we have been talking about. And probably in the last part, we will be seeking the boon."

"You predicted it, baby. We started by praising God with his overwhelming characteristics and then saluted him by focusing on HIM through meditation. And in the end, once we have elated the feeling of God being the supreme, we ask from him."

"So, what do we ask in this Mantra?"

"*Dhiyo* again used for intellect, and *Yo* means who or that. *Yo* is an 'indicator' or 'referred' to God and only HIM. The word

Nah, I feel brings the selfless part of the human being forward, means 'Ours' and this ours mean 'not only mine but everyone's', 'entire world's'."

"Okay. Here the enlightened intellect, through which we have focused on God, with various blissful characteristics, we seek something for the entire world; the world which we consider as our own and not separated from us."

"You got the right synopsis."

"Thanks. But what do we ask for? What is that we want it for all in this world? Everyone has different requirements and needs."

"All different requirements originate from one thing only, i.e. dis-satisfaction. And we are capable of overcoming it through our actions. The only requirement is that we get the right directions. *Prachodayat* means exactly that; guidance, direction and the path."

"So, this Mantra is all about spirituality only and does not have anything to do with our desires and wishes. In the end, when the time comes to solicit, we seek HIS guidance to take the right path and travel in the right direction. Maybe this is the reason why you feel so calm whenever you chant this Mantra."

"Yes. But your perception that it has nothing to do with our wishes and desire is wrong. The soul of the Mantra is *Savitur*, and by evoking *Savitur*, we can create anything we wish or desire. In this Mantra we are acknowledging that the supreme creator has bestowed the power of creation to us, and all we need is a mentor to guide us through. So, in the end, we request for what we lack, i.e. guidance, path and direction."

"Let me try a synopsis, I have noted down the meanings for my reference. *Gayatri* Mantra goes like this:

Starting with the 'so far secretive' sound of *Om,* the chanter remembers earth, air and sun as God. And then praises the Lord as supreme creator, the only one worthy to be followed as only He can purify us through His divine luminous light. A formless form where all the traits unite as one, and we meditate on him through our intellect. And through this connect during meditation; we seek guidance for all in the world."

"Beautiful. This is now strong autosuggestion for us to take away from selfishness and understand the piousness of the phrase *Vasudhaiva Kutumbkam,* entire world is one family. All the supreme characteristics of God inspire and empower us to be larger than what we consider ourselves today, as we too are the creators. And that feeling of gratitude makes us leave our ego and push us not to take the things for granted like earth, air and sun."

"I think this will be the first Mantra I will start chanting regularly and along with the meaning. I am not sure if I will be able to do it for 108 counts, but I will do for sure."

"Me too, I will try to make it a part of my pre-sleep and post-read activity. I won't even count the number, it would be a distraction. I will do it till I feel like and then sleep in the best feeling one could ever have. When I didn't know the meaning, even then this Mantra gave me so much solace, I am dying to experience the feeling when I do it with the meaning; reading it in my mind and voluntary picturing the visuals created by each word."

The pupil couple went down to practice the Mantra the same night. It was the way it had to be, wonderfully mood booster. That night they slept like infants, in their own world and completely different from the world around.

Aghorebhyo; At the Left Hand of Shiva

(Sample)

Chapter 1

It was the calmest night for her. Three days of exile had ended with all doubts scraped. She had a low blood pressure few days back, so it was not to happen again for weeks; that was the pattern. There was a festive mood with holidays in college and New Year nearing, she was insouciant as the coming morning would be commotion free. In a blue satin nightgown, her bare legs covered with a silky quilt, she was skimming the pages of her favorite book 'Delta Of Venus (1977) by Anais Nin'; she had missed it the most for the previous three nights. She read till her eyelids felt heavy, and she surrendered in the embrace of Hypnos.

In a deep swim of sleep, with no physical or emotional movement, she felt something placed on her stomach. It brought her back to being in no time. Still half-sleep she placed her right hand on her stomach and felt the same strange pressure on her hand as well. Right then, the doubts of Kabeer came back haunting her, and she was fully awake. She realised that her comforter was off, noodle strap of her nightgown was manipulated, and her right breast was impudently bare. The thought of someone's presence made her heart skip a beat. She decided to have a check and turned right to get up from the bed in a jiffy. She had just placed her right foot on the floor when she felt her left foot stuck, not in her quilt though. She couldn't stop her fall yet managed to balance herself with her hands on the ceramic tiles.

Her left foot that was still on the bed rose up in the air, and her satin nightgown slid up above her waist. She tried in vain to get back on the bed when the left foot rose further up, almost touching the fan; she was hung upside down. Her right foot limped in a perpendicular stance to the lifted one, with a painful stretch on the joint at the crotch. She was jostling with her hands aimlessly; her nightgown dropped beyond her chest, stuck in the armpits, and denuded her chubby body. Her hair hung straight, eyes flooded, "NO! PLEASE…" she screeched in dismay and cried for help. She was excruciatingly helpless.

Her hands were trying to hold on to something, her weak abdominal muscles were trying to crunch up to free her foot, and her wilting right foot was trying to pull back in its proper place.

Alas! All was futile.

Blood flowed to her head, tears flowing towards her hair, her face started to turn red, her brain was about to bust; dread struck her. She was being tortured in a sadist manner. With a loud scream, she broke and started weeping like a willow. Her tonsils felt inflamed, the saliva from her mouth started inching towards her eyes, and she begged to be released.

Her request was honored; just then the foot was set free, and her body fell on the floor with a thud. The shoulder was the first to hit the wooden floor, her knees were the last, the jerk got lot of liquid from her mouth and eyes to fall on the floor. Her tail bone hit the edge of the bed; it was for the fats on her hips and the eighteen-inch mattress that avoided a fracture. The hard impact on her torso made one of the ribs to swell-up, and she wailed in extreme pain. Her eyes and mouth were constantly flowing, there was no stopping to her acute crying and weeping.

A strong wind started to blow from the center of the room outwards. All the curtains found their way flying out of the window with their loops still in the rod. She was physically in severe pain, but she still had little hold left on her nerves. She tried getting up with the help of the side table. She was trying to hold on to it, but she had abated energy left than she thought, her quivering hands faltered, and she came down to the floor along with the table. Her knee got hurt and the pain added to her agony, she released another loud cry; she pulled her hair and scratched her face in anguish. Tears and saliva got mixed all over her face. She was sitting in the puddle of her own sweat, tears and saliva. Smitten with something beyond her comprehension she looked like a person who had lost sanity, and the way she was handled, she could go insane anytime.

The vase on the table, now stumbled, was broken, an alarm clock crushed, her photo-frame turned to smithers, and her mobile phone too was on the floor, but luckily safe. It was an old model and not one of the smart delicate ones. She grabbed it from the rubble and started dialing; few glass particles punctured her hands. She had just pressed the first key when her legs, again, were held tightly and pulled with the mightiest of a jerk. Her dress rode up till her shoulders and covered her face, extreme fear made her leak in her panty, but she held on to the phone tightly, and the same number key was kept pressing. Her naked body was pulled deeper in the room with more harshness, her back got bruised with pointed glass-bits blemishing the delicate flesh, and blood made its way out of the skin. Her nightgown was entirely off, her panty wedged-up, her body was sliding, and the skin got soiled in her own discharges. All this crushed her deep inside, she lost the sound of her crying, and the panic made her gasp for air.

She was held tight by her thighs and ankles and pressed hard on the floor. She didn't know that a call was initiated to the number saved on speed dial of the number key that was pressed for long; her moans and gasping sounds had been heard on the other side of the phone. With all the fragments of courage left she tried one last time to get out of the room, and out of the house. But she was being played in a savage taste, she felt too heavy below her waist as if mountains had been placed. She just could not move even an inch but was still trying to get on to something with her hands stretched towards the gaping door of her bedroom.

Unexpectedly in a forceful manner the main door of the house was flung open, it could be seen from where she was, and she spotted two angels. She tried to call them, but her voice was too meager, and then suddenly she saw a dark black ghost who was shouting at her; menacing her. She was already hell scared, but the ghost scared the life out of her. What happened next was a momentary loosening of the evil hold on her while one of the angels was pulling her; she used that as an opportunity to crawl out of the room and died.

It was only in the morning, in the hospital, she realised that though she had succumbed to the dreadful episode but wasn't dead.

She wasn't always in such a mess. Neither was she the only to be inflicted, albeit many more lives were inching towards an undesirable adventure. The seeds of their miseries were sown a year back when things were merry.

A year ago, somewhere in the city of Ahmedabad…

About the Author

Darpan Goyal is a self-proclaimed lover of life. He has three published books with fourth one around the corner. Along with books, he is a screenplay writer with around a dozen short films, web-series and also screenplays for songs out on the digital platforms.

You can reach him on twitter. His twitter handle is @ AuthorDarpan.